SECON

Jancy's first encounter with love and Saxon Marriot had brought nothing but pain, with his contemptuous rejection. A cruise seemed like an ideal break, a respite from the heartache . . . but Saxon was there, too, and there could be no escape from this shipbound second encounter . . .

SECOND ENCOUNTER

BY

MARGARET MAYO

MILLS & BOON LIMITED
15–16 BROOK'S MEWS
LONDON W1A 1DR

First published in Great Britain 1985
by Mills & Boon Limited

© Margaret Mayo 1985

Australian copyright 1985
Philippine copyright 1986
This edition 1986

ISBN 0 263 75252 6

Set in Monophoto Times 11 on 11 pt.
01–0186–52727

Made and printed in Great Britain by
Richard Clay (The Chaucer Press) Ltd,
Bungay, Suffolk

CHAPTER ONE

'I'M so happy I think I'm going to die.' Jancy threw herself down on the bed, locking her hands behind her head. 'I'm sure any day now Saxon will ask me to marry him.'

Ruth groaned and pulled the sheets over her face. 'Lucky you! Now let a girl get some sleep.'

But Jancy was far too elated to keep quiet, having just got in after her date. 'I think I must be the luckiest girl alive. I still can't believe that the eminent Saxon Marriot is in love with me.'

'I wish he wasn't,' grumbled Ruth, 'then we could both get some sleep. I'm sick of hearing his name.'

Jancy's smile deepened and she stretched her arms like a contented cat. 'Jealousy will get you nowhere.'

'You're suggesting I'm jealous?' Ruth sat up resignedly, hugging her hands round her knees. 'You're dead right, I am. Trust you to catch the best looking guy in the hospital. I still don't know how you did it. You must have something that the rest of us haven't.'

Gracefully Jancy pushed herself to her feet, sliding off her dress with slow sensual movements. She studied her reflection in the mirror. 'Venus has nothing on me.'

Her limbs were long and slender, her stomach flat, breasts high and firm. But she knew she was no great beauty. Her mouth was a little too wide, her nose too long. Her flaming copper hair was her crowning glory. Long and heavy, with the merest hint of a wave, it attracted attention wherever she went.

She turned away from the mirror, laughing, and knelt on the end of Ruth's bed. 'I honestly don't know why he's attracted to me. Sometimes I'm frightened. Everything's so perfect it can't last.'

It had been like that ever since she had met him at her sister's engagement party. She had recognised him immediately—the new consultant surgeon! There wasn't one nurse who did not entertain a secret passion for the handsome Mr Marriot, herself included. But he was a very aloof individual and never, ever, fraternised with the nurses.

Rumour had it that he was a widower and had not yet got over his wife's death. He certainly threw himself wholeheartedly into his work, never relaxing for one minute, his face hard and implacable at all times. He was an enigma, but none of the nurses believed that a man so vitally attractive could remain immune to the opposite sex for ever.

When Jancy spotted him he was surrounded by beautiful girls—all friends of her sister. And he was lapping it up! There was no sign of the ice-cold figure here.

His dark lounge suit contrasted strongly to the white hospital coat she was used to seeing him in. He looked different—more human. His crisp dark hair was neatly trimmed, defining his well-shaped head, emphasising the proud, arrogant angle of it.

From this distance Jancy could not see his eyes properly, but knew they were a cool steely blue, with the power to cut a person down to size without him so much as saying a word. Many a nurse had been reduced to tears with one withering glance. Always she had been careful never to do anything wrong in his presence—and so far had escaped his wrath.

His dark brows were angled in such a way that they almost peaked above his hawk-like nose, his mouth was firm, but his lower lip full and sensuous. Deep lines were scored from nose to mouth, suggesting life had not been easy. He was by far the most dominant male in the room and Jancy guessed there was not one woman present who would refuse to be his partner for the evening.

Yet he was not singling out any particular person. He was holding court, entertaining them all—until Jancy entered the room! His eyes moved in her direction almost as though her presence had been announced. She felt uncomfortable beneath his steady gaze and wished she had not let Ruth persuade her to wear this dress.

It had to be the dress that did it, otherwise he would not have taken a second glance. It was skin-tight in a blue-green iridescent material, cut low at both the back and front, slit to the thigh at one side.

'I'm fed up seeing you in those sedate little numbers you always wear,' Ruth had cried. 'Borrow this—it will do you a power of good. You know you usually feel insignificant in Kate's company.'

That was true. Jancy's flamboyant elder sister never did anything for her ego. She had the same gorgeous hair but the looks to go with it, and had overshadowed Jancy all her life. 'But it's Kate's party, it's her big night. I can't steal the limelight.'

'I doubt you'll do that,' said Ruth, 'knowing

Kate. Wear it—forget your inhibitions for once—
you're just as good as she is.'

And so Jancy had. She had literally felt that she
was being poured into the dress; it revealed every
curve and hollow, was the sexiest thing she had
ever worn—and she had felt exceptionally feminine—until she spotted Saxon Marriot. Now she
felt cheap.

She had brushed her waist-length hair until it
shone, sweeping it to one side and knotting it so
that it hung over one shoulder. To balance the
effect she wore a single earring with pearls and
lapis lazuli incorporated into silver filigree which
curved partly over her cheek and swept upwards
over her ear. The effect was stunning—or so Ruth
had assured her.

But Saxon Marriot's gaze was insolent and
assessing and Jancy moved uneasily. She felt as
though he was stripping her naked, looking right
through the beautiful material to her body
beneath. He eyed her up and down, quite slowly,
lingering on the shadowy vee between her breasts,
his eyes coming to rest at last on her face.

Jancy's cheeks coloured under his appraisal and
she felt an awareness she had never experienced
when seeing him at the hospital. He was different
tonight. They had always said what a fantastic
hunk of man he was, what an exciting male
animal—it had never been in dispute—but this
evening he was devastating!

And what was more, he found her attractive,
too. It was there in his eyes for all to see. Jancy
turned away and began talking to the person
standing next to her. But if anyone had asked her
what she was talking about she would not have
known, every fibre of her being was aware of

Saxon Marriot, she tingled with anticipation—a new feeling for Jancy.

She danced and smiled, laughed and joked, but all the time was aware that across the room a pair of powerful blue eyes were watching her. He was well over six feet and his muscled hardness was no longer hidden by the loose white hospital coat. He was a powerful man who walked tall, like some beautiful yet lethal jungle animal.

Seeing him in action tonight made her wonder whether the veneer of hardness he wore at the hospital was a façade. He had definitely never shown any interest in the female members of the staff. She had genuinely believed he was mourning the loss of his wife; now she began to wonder. He certainly had no hang-up at the moment.

She knew she ought to give him the cold shoulder, make it obvious that she was not interested. Whatever happened tonight he would ignore her at the hospital tomorrow. But it was as though he had hypnotised her, as though she was no longer capable of thinking for herself. Time and time again she looked towards him and on each occasion he gave her a wickedly seductive smile.

When her future brother-in-law asked her to dance Jancy said, 'How come Saxon Marriot is here? I've never heard you or Kate mention him. I wasn't aware that you were acquainted?'

'Of course,' laughed Philip, 'he works at the General, doesn't he? It never struck me that you two would know each other. He's an old mate of mine. We were at Oxford together. I haven't seen him in years. I bumped into him the other day and invited him to our party. He took a bit of persuading, but I must admit he looks as though he's enjoying himself.'

'I only know him by sight,' said Jancy. 'We've never actually been introduced.'

'I'll remedy that at once.' Without further ado Philip led her over to Saxon Marriot and his bevy of admirers.

'It doesn't matter,' protested Jancy, but he ignored her.

'Sax, old boy, meet Kate's sister, Jancy. She's a nurse at the General. I find it difficult to believe you've never met.'

The blue eyes were once again locked into hers. At close quarters Jancy could see that they were ringed with navy and had odd flecks in them which at this moment were very dark. His mouth widened into a slow reflective smile. 'I thought I recognised the face—but not the—er, body.' He held out his hand. 'I didn't realise we had such a beauty in that bunch of addle-headed nurses. Where have you been hiding yourself?'

If there was mockery in his voice Jancy chose to ignore it. Her heart was behaving in a most peculiar way. His hand was warm and firm and sent shivers dancing down her spine. There was an electric quality to the man that could not be ignored. She wondered whether every single girl here tonight was experiencing the same racing pulses.

'I don't think you've noticed any of us,' she said quietly, panic setting in as Philip left her to join his fiancée who had called from the kitchen. 'Except to chastise us if we do anything wrong.'

'Are you saying I've actually shouted—at you?' He sounded indecently shocked.

Jancy shook her head, her wide green eyes filling her face. She had no idea how breathtaking she looked. All she knew was that this man was causing her to breathe more quickly, her cheeks to glow with unaccustomed warmth. 'I've been careful.'

'You mean you've tried to ingratiate yourself into my good books?' There was a sudden sharpness to his tone, his eyes narrowed accusingly.

'I mean nothing of the kind,' returned Jancy defensively. He had no right speaking to her like that. He was not on duty now. How she wished she had never let Philip introduce her. She had made a mistake thinking he was different tonight.

His hands descended on her shoulders, calming, soothing, his smile for her alone. 'Don't get worked up, my little exotic butterfly. I have a naturally suspicious mind. You're quite the most captivating female I've seen in a long time.'

Jancy refused to believe that he was serious, eyeing him suspiciously, warily.

'Would you like to dance?' His voice was a low sexy growl and Jancy had the uneasy feeling that she was out of her depth. But she nodded—what else could she do?—and moved into his arms, closing her eyes as they swayed into a slow seductive waltz.

She felt an instant chemical response as he held her against his hard body. Her thighs brushed the long muscular length of his and his heart throbbed against her shoulder.

As she inhaled the intoxicating maleness of him Jancy knew she was lost. He wore an impossibly evocative aftershave, and there was the faint smell of cigar smoke on his breath as his lips moved against her hair.

Her heart beat a vital response and quite without realising what she was doing Jancy pressed closer. She had never felt this instant reaction to any man before and it both shocked and frightened her.

He wanted her, too. Each movement of his hard muscular body told her that. He found her the most desirable woman in the room, and she hungered after him with a wantonness that amazed her.

She was not even aware of the envious glances of the other girls, or her sister's curious frown, and when the dance ended and he swept her out into the garden she did not even give the room a backward glance.

His kisses held a magic that until this night Jancy had never experienced. He transported her into a world of sensation. Her whole body was vibrant with desire and she returned his kisses with an abandon that would have horrified her had she been in command of her senses.

Hungrily his hands explored her body, sliding her dress from her shoulders, claiming her breasts; stroking, tantalising, sending frissons of delight through her so that she felt as though she were about to faint from the sheer exquisite pleasure of it all.

Unashamedly she gave the total response his kisses demanded, running her hands over the smooth firmness of his body, feeling the ripple of muscle through the silk of his shirt, exhilarating over the intimate closeness of this sexy male animal.

She forgot who he was, that she would see him tomorrow and regret all this, closing her eyes, moaning softly as his kisses deepened, arching her body, knowing that she would quite willingly give herself to this man.

The primitiveness of her feelings shocked her. She had always vowed she would remain a virgin until she married yet here she was wanting Saxon Marriot, hungering for him, returning his kisses with an eagerness that clearly told him she was his for the taking.

Their lovemaking was finally disturbed when Jancy heard her name being called. It brought her back to her senses with a jolt. Her eyes snapped open and she looked at the handsome doctor in whose arms she was held so tightly. 'We must go back. This is madness.'

'Do you want to?' His voice was deep and sensual, coming from somewhere low in his throat. His black hair was silvered by the moonlight, his eyes in shadow, and his arms closed even more firmly about her.

Jancy shook her head. Even now, when she had this opportunity to escape, she did not want to. It was as though they were inextricably bound together. She belonged to him and he to her.

'Then don't,' he growled in her ear, his warm breath fanning her cheek. 'Let's go now, my car's waiting.'

'But my bag,' demurred Jancy.

'To hell with your bag,' he said thickly. 'You can collect it tomorrow. Tonight you belong to me.'

Such was the power of this man that Jancy allowed him to guide her towards the gleaming silver Mercedes that stood outside Kate's ground floor flat. He opened the door and handed her inside, making sure she was comfortable before walking round and sliding in himself.

The engine roared into life and Jancy sat back, closing her eyes. This was sheer madness. She was out of her mind. Yet the way he had said, *Tonight you belong to me* made her realise that arguing would be futile—and did she want to anyway?

She was here of her own volition, her pulses throbbing furiously, her whole body alive with a sexuality that was alien to her. She could blame no one but herself for what was about to happen.

In profile his forehead was high and noble, his black brows jutting, his chin strong and uncompromising. He looked arrogant, sophisticated, and very confident. He was that way on the wards. But then he was also unapproachable. Tonight he was different. He was human—and he was hungry for her!

Sensing her interest he turned his head, his slow smile encompassing her, making love to her. He touched her arm and it was as though an electric current ran through her. She shivered involuntarily, but lifted his hand to her mouth, pressing a kiss into his palm before giving it back to him.

He looked pleased by her reaction. Before long he pulled up outside an exclusive apartment block. Still in her dream world Jancy accompanied him inside. They were whisked up in a high-speed lift to his penthouse suite. She supposed she ought to have known he lived somewhere like this.

As soon as the door to his apartment closed he turned and took her hungrily into his arms. Jancy's whole body throbbed with a frenzy of excitement. She returned his kisses freely, her lips parting, accepting his probing tongue, making no demur when he slid her dress from her shoulders.

It was not until he swept her up into his arms and carried her through into his bedroom that a thread of sanity crept in. Even then she did not have the power to call a halt to the proceedings. He had completely taken over her body.

He lay her down on the bed, standing back and surveying her enigmatically. 'God, but you're beautiful.'

Jancy had never had a man look at her naked body before and although instinct made her want to cross her arms in front of her, her need for him made her throw inhibitions to the wind. She felt proud that he should find her desirable. Her breasts ached and throbbed, her stomach was a chaos of emotion, and she wanted him more than anything in the world.

'I can't think how I overlooked you at the hospital,' he continued, as he hurriedly began to undress. 'You attracted me from the moment I spotted you at your sister's party.'

Jancy's heart throbbed painfully as she watched his trousers join his shirt on the back of a chair. His limbs were long, hard and tightly muscled. He had a lithe grace, an ease of movement that reminded her yet again of the jungle animal she had likened him to earlier. There was not an ounce of superfluous flesh on him and she feasted her eyes on his magnificence.

The longed for moment arrived when he lay down beside her. She turned instinctively, willingly, into his arms. It did not strike her as strange that she was giving herself to a man who, until tonight, had been nothing more than a name. This whole affair meant more to her than that—and to him, she was sure.

Tonight would not be the be all and end all of their relationship. It would develop into something sweeter than life itself. She did not know why she felt so sure but it was as though their meeting had been preordained. She and Saxon were made for each other.

The feel of his hair-roughened skin against her breasts was yet another unique experience. She arched herself against the pulsating hardness of his body, accepting and returning his fierce demandding kisses. There was a hunger in him that could not be denied, and a powerful response inside herself. Their body chemistry said it all for them. There was no need for words. He was not a stranger but a natural partner. They belonged. It was an inexplicable, wonderful feeling.

She pondered whether this was the first time he had been with another woman since his wife died. She hoped so. She would do all in her power to help him forget his sadness. Show him that he still had a life to live and that she was prepared to make him happy.

His movements were eager and passionate, yet not savage. His kisses were demanding, but she knew she had only to say the word and he would stop. Not that she wanted him to. She wanted these moments to go on for ever. It was the sweetest most exhilarating experience of her life. Her whole body felt as though it were about to explode. White hot heat travelled through each and every limb, setting her on fire, causing her to cling to him as moans of erotic pleasure surfaced from deep in her throat.

Spirals of delight curled through her as he took the rosy peaks of her breasts into his mouth, his hands moving expertly over her body until she was sure he must know her as intimately as she knew herself.

'Make love to me,' she whispered when she could stand it no longer. He was driving her insane. 'Please make love to me now.'

With a savage cry he thrust her from him and Jancy was left cold and petrified staring up into the harsh brutality of his face. 'What have I done?'

'Done?' he crazed. 'When I make love it's because I want to, not because some sex-mad young woman begs me to. I'd hoped I was mistaken, that I'd misread the invitation in your eyes, the promises of your body. I should have known that anyone wearing a dress like yours couldn't be expected to have any morals. You picked on the wrong person, though, Miss Jancy Ullman, when you set your sights on me. I prefer to do the chasing myself.'

'But I wasn't, I didn't——' Jancy listened with growing horror to his tirade. 'Please, Saxon—Mr Marriot—it wasn't like that at all——'

'Like what?' he sneered, lips curling as he pulled on the trousers he had discarded with seeming willingness only minutes earlier. His movements now were tempered with anger, jerky, unsteady, his fingers clawing at the fine material.

'I thought that—you—felt the same? You gave the impression that you wanted it as much as me.' Jancy was appalled to feel hot tears slide down her cheeks and dashed them away angrily with the back of her hand.

'Oh, I wanted you all right,' he snarled. 'I still do. You're very sexy and very desirable—you're also a bitch. Get the hell out of here before I lose control altogether.' His face was flushed and ugly now, contorted with a passion that was gnawing away at his sanity.

'I demand the right to defend myself,' cried Jancy, snatching at a sheet and clutching it against her trembling body. 'I'm not like that at all. You have it wrong. I've never solicited a man in my life.'

His head jerked. 'Are you denying that you deliberately gave me the eye across that room tonight?'

'You looked at me,' she whispered painfully. 'It was you who called the tune.'

'I was admiring a beautiful woman. I was not saying come to bed.'

'Neither was I.' Her voice grew lower and she shook so violently her nervous fingers could barely hold the sheet. 'I've never felt this way before. I thought it was something special and rare— something that you felt, too.' Her eyes filled with tears. 'I'm sorry if I unwittingly misled you. It was not my intention.' She looked down at her hands, unable to face him any longer. She felt cheap and humiliated—and wished with all her heart that she had never gone to Kate's party.

'You sound very convincing,' he snarled, 'but it doesn't fool me. I fell for the oldest trick in the book.' He sounded disgusted with himself, his face ablaze with savage anger, his eyes ignited into white hot flames. 'Perhaps I ought to take advantage? Perhaps I ought to finish the job? I could sure do with a woman right now.'

Jancy recoiled, her hands flying to her mouth. She did not want him to take her in anger. Her green, wide, petrified eyes were like twin jewelled orbs above her fists, there was a pain in her chest as she fought for breath.

'Frightens you, does it?' he sneered, advancing slow inch by slow inch. 'But wasn't this what you wanted? I'm fully aware that I'm regarded as unattainable. No doubt you thought it would be a feather in your cap. My God, I've a good mind to give you something to remember me by, and it sure as hell won't be pleasant.'

His weight on the edge of the bed caused Jancy to roll towards him. She snatched back in alarm, fearing now for her safety. There was a manic quality about him. Gone was the tenderness, the caring. He wanted to hurt her—and badly.

'I didn't proposition you,' she protested faintly, watching in growing horror as he plucked the protective sheet away. 'If I read you wrongly, I'm sorry. I certainly never had any intention of——'

'Going to bed with me?' he cut in thickly, harshly. 'Hell, I never saw you protesting. You're the easiest——'

Jancy could not listen to his insinuations a moment longer. She swung her arm in a wide arc and slapped him hard and satisfyingly across one cheek. 'Don't speak to me like that, Mr Marriot. I'm as good as you any day. My only mistake was in thinking you were attracted to me. I thought our feelings were mutual. It was a mistake I shall regret for the rest of my life.'

She turned away, leaping from the bed and dashing through into the other room where her clothes still lay on the floor. It went against the grain to pull on the offending dress which was the indirect cause of her downfall.

But Saxon Marriot was behind her even before she had picked it up, his hands on her shoulders, spinning her to face him. He said nothing, simply searching her face, a faint frown drawing his black winged brows together so that they appeared like an eagle in flight. He was looking for something, delving into her soul, her mind.

Jancy quivered but held her chin up bravely. The red imprint of her hand on his cheek gave her a certain satisfaction—and she had nothing to hide. Her eyes were clear as she looked into his.

He groaned suddenly, his hooded lids falling, shutting in a pain she only briefly glimpsed. He pulled her against the tense hardness of his body and Jancy felt a tremor run through him.

'It looks as though it was me who made the mistake,' he said hoarsely. 'You're too upset to be playing a part. Can you ever forgive me?' He took her face between his hands, his thumbs gently stroking away the trace of tears.

She smiled weakly, aware that her lower lip was trembling. It was foolish to forgive him yet she could not help herself. He had wounded her pride yet she did not hate him. In a way she was at fault, she ought not to have been so eager.

'I can understand you feeling the way you did,' she said shyly. 'I got rather carried away.' Which was an understatement to say the least. Her emotions had washed over her in an unstemmable tide. There had been nothing she could do. Only this man's harsh reaction had brought her to her senses. Maybe it had been a blessing in disguise?

He lowered his head and kissed her mouth gently. 'I think I'd better take you home.'

She nodded miserably and there was silence between them as they put on their once eagerly discarded clothes.

Outside the nurses' home Saxon took her hand gravely and raised it to his lips. Jancy felt sad, What had promised to be an exciting and fulfilling evening had turned out a disaster. 'Goodbye,' she whispered huskily.

'Not goodbye,' he said. 'I misjudged you—and that's a pity. But I'd like to see you again—if you can possibly bear the sight of me?'

It was difficult to read his expression in the dark but he sounded sincere. 'I would like to,' she admitted, knowing she was all kinds of a fool, but still feeling an unaccountable attraction.

'Good,' he said. 'We'll go out for a meal some time. Would you like that?'

Jancy nodded. It would be infinitely safer than going to his flat again—and she would be extra careful in future never to give him the wrong impression. She had learned her lesson.

He watched as she let herself in. She paused a moment, listening as the purr of his car faded into nothingness, then crept into the room she shared with Ruth, careful not to wake her. Without bothering to put on the light, or even to wash off her make-up, she slipped out of the hateful dress and into bed.

But she could not sleep. Her mind was constantly on Saxon Marriot. It had been quite an eventful evening one way and another. She had seen both the brutal and tender side of him—and knew which she preferred.

Was there any point in developing a relationship? she wondered. Wouldn't he always entertain a faint doubt that she was not as virtuous as she declared? It was a demoralising thought.

She and Ruth were both on duty early and as neither were at their best first thing in a morning nothing was said about the party, for which Jancy was grateful. Her meeting with the doctor was something she wanted to keep to herself for the time being. Discounting his accusations it was far too magical an experience to be shared.

But when they got to the hospital she discovered that everyone knew. Some super-sleuth had seen her getting into his car—and no sooner had she entered the staff room than there was a chorus of voices.

'You dark horse!'

'Come on, let's hear what happened.'

'How on earth did you manage it?'

'You've certainly won the bet.'

'God, that stupid bet!' cried Jancy. 'I never gave it a thought.' It was something that had been dreamed up months ago when Saxon Marriot first came to the hospital.

He was quite the handsomest doctor they'd ever had working there. But he was aloof. They could have been non-existent for all the notice he took. He had them scurrying around after him like little slaves, but he did not remember any one of them by name. It was just, 'Nurse, do this. Nurse, do that.' He earned himself a reputation for being totally disagreeable.

It was not until he had been at the hospital for some time that they learned he was a widower, and Jancy remembered thinking that he must have loved his wife very much. In his unguarded moments there was pain behind his eyes, though it was not often he let his veneer slip.

And then Linda had come up with the hare-brained scheme that they try to break down Mr Marriot's reserve. She cut a picture of him from a local newspaper and framed it with cardboard. 'This,' she declared grandly, 'is the trophy for the first girl who dates Saxon Marriot.'

They all knew it was well nigh impossible—but it was a nice thought all the same, and they spent long minutes staring at the photograph. Even in black and white his sexuality was indisputable.

The dark eyes staring out from the page were mysterious and disturbing, and it was easy to imagine them piercing into you as he whispered tender words of love. They all entertained day dreams, Jancy amongst them, but they also knew it was unlikely he would ever notice any of them, yet alone take them out.

'You mean you didn't deliberately set out to ensnare him?' asked Linda.

Jancy shook her head. 'No way. He was at my sister's engagement party, would you believe? He's an old friend of my future brother-in-law.'

'And he just walked up and made a pass at you, I suppose?' enquired Ruth.

They all laughed, knowing how ridiculous this was.

'As a matter of fact,' said Jancy, it was something like that. It was your dress that did it, Ruth. He just kept looking at me. He didn't even know I was one of his nurses. Lord, I thought his eyes were going to pop out.' She tossed her head and gave a twirl. 'He said I was like an exotic butterfly.'

There were swoons all round.

'Did he kiss you?'

'What was it like?'

'Oh, come on, Jancy, do tell us. I'd die if it happened to me.'

The comments were thick and furious. Jancy turned away angrily. Shut up, all of you. He's a very nice man.'

'But of course you'd say that,' said Linda. 'Wouldn't any one of us who'd been out with him. Some people have all the luck. Where did you go? Did he take you back to his place? Here—you've won this. Stand it by your bed so that you can gaze into his eyes before falling asleep.'

Jancy took the picture and studied it. Simply looking at his face, which was really not a very good likeness, made her heartbeats quicken; a

longing surged through her and she could not wait
to see him again.

All day she hoped to catch a glimpse of him, but
he did not put in an appearance. She could only
assume it was his day off. She desperately wanted
to talk to him, find out about him. They had
spoken so little. They had not discussed each
other. All they had been interested in were their
bodies. Jancy felt deeply shocked at the animal
hunger that had made her offer herself to him—
the cause of him doubting her moral values.

Did this really happen? Could she feel such a
physical attraction at first sight? It did not seem
possible—and yet it had happened. He filled her
every thought. For the first time that day she
almost administered the wrong medicine, causing
Sister to reprimand her sharply.

Back in the flat Jancy placed the picture almost
reverently on the table beside her bed. Ruth asked
the same question that had been in her mind. 'Are
you seeing him again?'

Jancy shrugged. 'I think so.'

'I wish you'd woken me last night and told me
about it. Gosh, I'd give my eye teeth to be kissed
by him. What was he like? Is he as sexy as he
looks?'

'Wrap it up, Ruth,' said Jancy. 'I don't want to
talk about it.' Her feelings for Saxon were private.
She wanted to discuss him with no one.

Several days passed and although Jancy saw
him at the hospital it was always from a distance.
He made no effort to seek her out and she began
to wonder whether he had changed his mind about
seeing her again.

Perhaps he had thought the whole thing over
and decided that she had been lying after all, that

she had been inviting his advances. The thought hurt. She guessed she would never live down the reputation he had so cruelly pinned on her.

And then, when she was least expecting it, he turned up outside the nurses' home. She was just about to go inside when his car swooped to a halt in front of her.

'Hurry and get changed,' he said. 'I'm taking you out.'

It was an order, not an invitation, and Jancy stared at him for a full minute without answering.

'What's wrong?' he asked impatiently, his blue eyes flashing. 'Don't you want to come?'

'Yes, I'd love to. It was just a—shock, that's all. Will you come in and wait while I get ready?'

He shook his head brusquely. 'I have business to attend. I'll be back in twenty minutes. Can you make it in that time?'

She nodded eagerly. 'Of course. Where are we going? What shall I wear?'

'For a meal,' he said. 'Wear something smart and not too revealing.' His lips twisted wryly. 'I don't want you to be ogled by every other man.'

He need have no fear she would ever wear a dress like that again, thought Jancy as she skipped inside, her heart singing. She was glad Ruth was still on duty, imagining the questions that would have been fired.

She felt wonderfully, magically, vibrantly alive. As the days slipped by she had given up hope that Saxon Marriot would ask her out again. And now he had. It meant he had accepted that she had not deliberately flung herself at him. Wasn't the world a marvellous place?

She surveyed the contents of her wardrobe ruefully. Something smart, he had said. None of her clothes were really elegant, not the sort to wear at one of the top restaurants he would surely choose. The minutes ticked away and she still could not make up her mind.

She looked through Ruth's wardrobe, knowing her friend would not mind her borrowing. But Ruth was an entirely different personality, loving to wear clothes that shocked or drew attention to herself. 'It's bad enough wearing a uniform when I'm on duty,' she moaned. 'In my free time I have to let go.'

Her clothes, therefore, were bizarre and colourful, not at all the sort of thing that Saxon would approve. But pushed at the back was a sunny yellow blouse that Ruth never wore. Jancy dragged it out. It would liven up that bronze suit she had once bought in a fit of madness and then decided it did nothing for her.

There was precious little time left and after a quick shower Jancy dragged on her clothes with hands that were distinctly shaky.

The yellow blouse enlivened the suit perfectly and she brushed out her hair, braiding it expertly, coiling it in a coronet on top of her head. She applied very little make-up, a hint of eye shadow and a trace of lipstick, that was all. It was important she create the right impression.

When she heard his horn blare impatiently she took one last look at herself, satisfied he could not fault her appearance tonight.

Even so her smile was hesitant as she climbed in beside him, her heart hammering loud enough for him to hear. His blue eyes surveyed her slowly, observing the heightened colour in her cheeks, the brightness of her eyes, smiling at the frilled high neck of the blouse, the neat skirt which demurely covered her knees.

'Very proper,' he said, a wicked glint in his eyes, 'but also very becoming. It hints beautifully at the sexy woman beneath. You're even lovelier than I remember.'

And he was more intoxicating! He had on a navy pin-striped suit with a pale blue shirt and maroon tie, a matching handkerchief tucked into his top pocket. He looked excitingly male and she could not drag her eyes away.

'What are you thinking?' His smile deepened.

'Just how lucky I am.' There was no way she could ignore the sexual magnetism that attracted her to him.

His brows rose. 'Lucky?'

'That you've given me a second chance.'

His eyes darkened and he put his hands on her shoulders, withdrawing instantly, savagely. 'Hell, this is neither the time nor the place. I want to feel you in my arms again, do you know that?'

The car shot forward and Jancy observed his hands tight on the wheel.

'I've lain awake at night and thought of nothing but you. It's crazy, isn't it? What is it about you, Jancy, that's got beneath my skin?'

'It's one of those odd things that happen, I suppose,' she said shyly, knowing that she felt the same but not daring to admit it. She must never appear too eager again. At least not until she was sure of him.

He took her to a very small but very exclusive restaurant where he knew the waiters by their first names. They lingered over their meal and all the time they were eating he did not take his eyes off her.

Jancy felt she was being devoured, that he was making mental love to her, and her emotions were at fever pitch by the time they had finished their coffee and he suggested they leave.

She wondered whether he would take her back to his flat, whether there would be a repetition of the other night's lovemaking? Except that this time she would not offer herself so freely.

It was the biggest disappointment of her life when he drove straight back to the nurses' home. Her eyes were wide as she looked at him in the darkness of the car.

He took her hands. 'It has to be this way. I can't trust myself with you.' She could feel him trembling. 'If I so much as kiss you I shan't be able to stop. Can you understand that, Jancy? You're potent, like a heady wine. You've got beneath my skin like no other woman has since——' He stopped. A shutter came over his eyes and he released her hands. 'Please go.'

Jancy felt choked by the abruptness of his tone. 'Good night then,' she husked, 'and thank you for a pleasant evening.'

She almost threw herself out of the car, racing into the nurses' home without bothering to close the car door behind her. She ought not to feel hurt, she should feel sad—for Saxon's sake. But she could not help it. He was letting the shadowy figure of his wife come between him and any chance of future happiness. It was not right he should dwell on her memory for ever. He had to begin again.

But at least this was a start. She was, if all accounts were true, the first girl he had dated since his wife's death. He was certainly finding it difficult to let go, but she was sure he would in time. He had admitted how deeply attracted he was to her. All she had to do was be patient.

When Jancy burst into her nurses' home room Ruth was curled up in an armchair reading a magazine. 'Hi! Where have you been? No, don't tell me, let me guess. Out with our sexy doctor friend?'

Jancy nodded, there was no point in denying it. 'I borrowed your blouse, I hope you don't mind?'

'You can have it,' exclaimed Ruth. 'I never liked the thing anyway. It's too—ordinary. It suits you, though—very chaste. What did our Mr Marriot think of the transformation?'

'He approved,' said Jancy with pretended haughtiness.

'I bet that's not all he did.' Ruth's sooty black eyes were dancing. 'You look as though you're in love.'

'I think perhaps I am,' said Jancy. 'I never knew it could happen so quickly.'

'And our eminent friend, does he return your feelings?'

Jancy's face shadowed. 'I don't know. I think he's still mourning his wife. He finds me attractive, but she somehow got in the way.'

'It's natural he'll compare you,' said Ruth. 'But what the hell, he can't live in the past for ever. At least he's interested, that's the main thing. I reckon you'll have him eating out of your hand in no time at all.'

Jancy never knew when Saxon was going to invite her out. She could go for days without seeing him, then he would appear outside the nurses' home when she was least expecting it. The fact that they both worked irregular hours made it difficult, and if ever they met inside the hospital he would give her no more than a tight, polite smile, which said, I never mix business with pleasure. At first it hurt, but gradually Jancy grew to accept it. If this was the way Saxon Marriot wanted things then so be it.

Occasionally, very occasionally, they went back to his flat, and then his lovemaking was tempered with savagery. Jancy did not mind. He was a very exciting lover and she in her turn discovered that she possessed a far deeper capacity for loving than she had ever suspected. She felt at times like a primitive woman and was often frightened by the depth of her feelings. But he always stopped long before things got out of control and she in her turn was always careful to hold back, never to reveal too deeply how she felt.

Only once did she question Saxon about his wife. 'You must have loved her very much. What was she like?'

'Who told you about my wife?' he crashed harshly, his face creased in an anguish she had not seen before.

Jancy stepped back in amazement. 'It's common knowledge you're a widower, but you're so secretive about it I don't think anyone has the nerve to ask you.'

'And you think that you're different? You think that because I've taken you out a few times it gives you the right to pry into my private life?'

Jancy felt as though she had been slapped. 'I'm not prying. I thought that we were close enough for you to be able to talk about it.'

'I don't want to discuss my wife—ever,' he snarled. 'Is that clear?'

She gulped and nodded. Saxon in this mood was disconcerting. He became a virtual stranger. Again that arrogant individual who prowled the hospital corridors, intimidating the nurses. 'I'm sorry,' she said, 'I won't mention her again.'

The next time he took her out he was as charming as ever and it was easy for Jancy to forget how angry he had been. But she did wonder why he refused to discuss his wife. She could only think that the memory of her was still too painful. He would feel better if he did, she was sure, but he would never listen to advice from her—or anyone else.

They were soon seeing each other on every possible occasion, and Jancy began to feel confident in their relationship. Everything was perfect—their lovemaking, friendship, the whole lot. He had not actually said that he loved her but she could tell, and she was sure she must be the happiest woman in the world.

As she said to Ruth, it was so perfect it was frightening. And then the bubble burst! She was in her shared room one day when the door crashed open, pushed so violently that the wood splintered around the lock.

Saxon stood there like a man demented, his face flushed an ugly red, his eyes glacial, almost bulbous, his fingers curled into his palms as if only by a supreme effort was he able to keep them off her.

Jancy's green eyes widened anxiously, her mouth suddenly tinder-dry. 'What's wrong?'

He pounced on her then, his fingers digging into the soft flesh of her upper arms; bruising, hurting, making her want to cry out. 'No one makes a fool of me and gets away with it.' Muscles worked in his jaw as he savagely shook her.

There was something maniacal about him—and Jancy feared for her life. He had been angry before, that first day in his apartment, but it was nothing compared to the rage that burned in him now.

CHAPTER TWO

'I DON'T know what you're talking about.' Jancy struggled futilely to escape.

'Don't you?' Saxon's face was hard and uncompromising. 'My God, how neatly you had me fooled. How you must have laughed up your sleeve.'

Jancy was bewildered. 'Let me go, you brute. I really don't know what you mean. How have I fooled you? What have I done this time?' The more she struggled the deeper his fingers bit until the pain became unbearable.

'As if you don't know.' His lips curled damningly and he pushed her away from him so violently that she fell backwards against the wall.

The impact knocked the breath from her body and for what seemed like minutes, but must have been only seconds, she stood there, finding it difficult to believe that this insane monster was the same man in whose arms she had lain so willingly, who had treated her with tender passion that had thrilled her to the core. 'Perhaps you'd tell me what it is I'm supposed to have done?'

His eyes narrowed menacingly. 'Do you deny that you *won me*—in a bet?' The harsh guttural tones of his voice ricocheted through the room. Jancy suspected that everyone in the building could hear.

Her change of expression gave him the answer he needed. He pounced triumphantly. 'I see I am right. I didn't realise I was the centre of so much attention. What a star you must be. Do you relay every intimate detail of our embraces to your fellow nurses? Is that it? Is that where you get your kicks? God, you make me sick!' He flung away in disgust, his face distorted grotesquely, his whole body rejecting her.

Such was the venom in his tone that Jancy flinched as though she had been struck. A cold sweat broke out and she trembled so violently that she was forced to claw the wall behind her for support. 'There was a bet,' she admitted quietly, 'but me meeting you had nothing to do with it.'

'Oh, no?' he sneered. 'Are you trying to say that it was all coincidence that Phil invited me to his engagement party? That you did not deliberately set out to seduce me that evening in order to gloat to your friends and win the coveted trophy?'

'No, I didn't, *I didn't*,' cried Jancy passionately. 'Please, Saxon, you must believe me.' She walked over to him, but he turned away as though even the sight of her was too much.

'I believed you once,' he said, 'but never again. Whatever you say, whatever lies you conjure up, it will make no difference.'

'But, Saxon, you can't condemn me without giving me an opportunity to defend myself.' Jancy's heart pounded so painfully that she clutched at it, one hand clasped on top of the other beneath her breast, her eyes wide and anguished, filling her face.

'Can't I?' He swung round and she caught her breath at the total savagery of him. 'I gave you the benefit of the doubt once. You fooled me completely with those big shiny eyes, that trembling mouth. A very convincing display, my little—*slut*. You're in the wrong profession, do you know that? Go on the stage and you'll be a winner. But you'll never fool me again. I was the biggest sucker of them all. I fell for your professed innocence. Wasn't that a laugh?'

'I am innocent,' she cried despairingly. 'What must I say to make you believe it?'

'There is nothing you can say.' His cold blue eyes pierced her as effectively as if they had been twin blades of steel. She felt the cutting edge of his venom with an actual physical pain. 'If you'd told me about the competition, admitted that you'd won it inadvertently, them we might have both had a laugh, I might just have believed you. But your very silence is your executioner. You've been found guilty, my dear Jancy, and there is not one damn thing you can do about it.'

'You mean that whatever I say will make no difference? That you prefer to believe what others have told you instead of listening to me?'

'I listened once,' he said.

'And rightly so. Oh, Saxon, why do you doubt me?' She ventured towards him but was stopped by the intense loathing on his face. It was as though he had erected a barrier between them. She must penetrate it. She had done no wrong. She had to make him believe that. Her future, her whole life, depended on it. She loved Saxon. She could not let him walk out thinking the worst of her.

'Nothing was planned,' she said softly. 'Ask Kate, ask Phil. I wasn't even aware that Phil knew you. And that lousy bet was never intended to be serious. It was a giggle. We all knew there was not the remotest chance that you'd ever notice any one of us.'

'Not unless you paraded in front of me in next to nothing,' he thrust malevolently. 'I'm only human, Jancy, in case it has escaped your notice.'

'I borrowed my friend's dress, for heaven's sake. It was her idea. Neither of us knew you were going to be there. I'm not the sexy siren you seem to think. I'm a very ordinary girl who made the mistake of falling in love with a man who is not capable of seeing any deeper than the surface. If you could you would see that I'm sincere. It was no game. I love you, Saxon, it's as simple as that.'

Doubt appeared on his face and Jancy knew she was winning. 'Don't you see,' she persisted, 'someone's trying to cause trouble. Everyone's jealous of the interest you're showing in me.' She stretched her arm out towards him, but he was not ready for that yet and turned away quickly.

'I want to believe you, Jancy. I don't like what I've heard, but——' He stopped, his eyes alighting on the photograph on Jancy's bedside table. He stilled dangerously before he snatched it up, shoving it mercilessly beneath her nose. 'No part in the bet, eh? So what are you doing with this? It is the prize, isn't it? I've heard all about this famous picture of me.' He tore it across the middle, again and again, finally flinging the pieces in her face. 'Don't—ever—let—me—see—you—again.' He emphasised each word to add impact.

Jancy made a half step towards him. 'But——'

'But nothing,' he snapped. 'It's all over. You very nearly had me fooled yet again. You're clever, Jancy, I'll hand you that, and I'm a prize fool.' He gave her one last scathing glance before storming out, banging the door so violently that the injured frame creaked protestingly and the door swung drunkenly back open.

With tears racing down her cheeks Jancy called after him. 'Saxon, please, you must listen. You have it all wrong.' But he had gone. There was no one to hear except the other occupants of the nurses' home.

So that was the end. He would not even let her defend herself. She couldn't believe that he would react in this manner after the very special hours they had spent together. There had been a rapport between them that she had felt with no other man, and he had given the impression that he felt that way too. Surely he would not let idle gossip warp his mind?

She would give him time to calm down and then go to see him, make him believe that she had nothing to do with that stupid bet, that the picture had been forced on her, and because of the way she felt about him it had seemed natural to stand it beside her bed.

There were still traces of tears on her face when Ruth arrived back, looking questioningly at the splintered door frame. 'What's happened?'

'I had a row with Saxon,' said Jancy despondently. 'We're finished. It's all over.'

'I don't believe it.' Ruth's dark eyes shot wide. 'You told me only yesterday that you thought he'd be asking you to marry him.'

Jancy shrugged. 'He now thinks I'm the lowest of the low. His opinion of me has dropped to zero. It's a wonder I'm still in one piece.'

Ruth glanced at the shreds of newspaper still littering the floor. 'What have you been doing, getting him out of your system?'

'He did that,' said Jancy loudly.

'For pity's sake,' returned Ruth, 'you'd better tell me about it.'

Jancy looked resigned. 'He heard about that silly bet, would you believe? I don't know who told him.'

'And he thinks that you——'

Jancy nodded. 'He wouldn't even listen. I didn't tell you before, but on that first day we met he accused me of trying to seduce him. I wasn't, you know me better than that, I was simply following the dictates of my heart. I suppose it must have looked like it, especially me wearing that dress. It certainly taught me a lesson. I shall never let another man know what I feel, not until I'm sure of him. I thought I'd convinced Saxon, but now he's heard about that ridiculous wager he thinks I've been lying all along. It's over, Ruth. He said he never wants to see me again.'

'Huh!' said Ruth bitterly. 'Quite how he'll manage that I don't know. You're sure to bump into each other.'

'I know,' admitted Jancy dully. 'I'll have to leave.'

'Leave? What the hell for? Don't let him frighten you away. You've done no wrong so hold your head up high. Who does he think he is, anyway?'

Jancy smiled wryly. 'He's the man I love.'

'He's not worthy of your love,' returned her friend sharply. 'I'd like to say forget him, but I know that won't be easy. But for God's sake don't let him make you give up all you've worked for. You like it here, you know you do.'

'I'm going to give him a few days to cool down,' said Jancy, 'then I'm going round to his flat. Even if we don't get back together I must clear things up. I can't live with this cloud over me.'

It crucified Jancy to have Saxon ignore her

completely in the days that followed. There was no sign at all of his anger lessening. She came to the sad conclusion that it meant he did not love her. He couldn't do, otherwise he would have listened to her side of the story.

After a week of little or no sleep Jancy decided the time had come to go and see him. Her heart was racing fit to burst when she approached the apartment block where he lived.

The main doors to the building were locked and she hung around hoping to slip inside with someone else. But no one came and in the end she was forced to ring Saxon. His voice came through the grille.

'It's Jancy,' she said. 'I want to see you.'

'Do you?' Even though his voice was muffled she could hear the hardening of his tone. 'Well, I don't want to see you. Haven't I made myself clear?'

'You must listen to me,' she said. 'I want to explain.'

'Are you saying that you did not win that bet?'

'The girls said I did, but——'

'Then that's good enough for me. Goodbye, Jancy.'

At that moment a young woman, whom Jancy had seen a couple of times, entered the building. 'Are you coming up?' she asked cheerfully, 'save you waiting for your young man to let you in.'

Jancy did not stop to consider the consequences. This thing had to be thrashed out. In seconds she had reached his penthouse suite and knocked the door firmly, determined to let him intimidate her no longer.

It was yanked wide. He stood there tall and indomitable, his white shirt open to the waist, black trousers sitting low on his sexy hips, moulding the hard length of thigh. His hair was damp and curled crisply as though he had just come out of the shower. He looked fresh and vital—and certainly not as though he had lost any sleep over her.

'You!' he stabbed, a frown cutting between his brows. 'How did you get in? Didn't I make myself clear?'

'Eminently,' she said quietly, aware of the need to keep calm, 'but you must give me a chance.'

'Why must I?'

'Because I——' It was then that Jancy caught sight of a woman hovering in the background. She had her back to the door and was pouring drinks into two glasses that were set out on a tray. Her hair was silver blonde. She was tall, slim and elegant, and wore a black evening dress that was cut as low, if not lower, than the one Jancy had worn to Kate's party.

Jancy's words stuck in her throat. He had certainly lost no time in consoling himself with another woman. She tore her eyes away and looked at him painfully. 'I reckon I made a mistake.' She swung away and began to retrace her steps, stifling a cry at the injustice of it all.

His door closed but not before she had heard Saxon's low voice and the woman laughing in response. Were they laughing at her? She guessed so. This really was the end. Saxon had made it perfectly clear that he wanted nothing more to do with her, and she would not lower herself by imploring him yet again to hear her side of the story.

When she got back to her room in the nurses' home she decided that the only sane thing to do was leave the hospital. It was not what she wanted, but she could never be happy here again. Not with Saxon Marriot stalking the corridors. There was no saying when their paths would cross—and he would take great pleasure in cutting the ground from beneath her feet, in humiliating her, in showing her up in front of his colleagues and patients alike.

She had some holiday due and decided to use this in lieu of notice. She could not risk remaining at the hospital any longer, not if she wanted to stay sane. Ruth tried to dissuade her but Jancy remained stubborn. 'I just can't, Ruth. It's impossible. I shall be a nervous wreck if I carry on. He's destroying me.'

Private nursing appealed to her and although she had never intended trying it until she was older, Jancy felt it might be the answer now. She scoured the advertisements in *The Lady* and eventually got an interview with a Mrs Fairfax, who turned out to be a kind elderly woman with thick white well-kept hair and twinkling blue eyes. Jancy took to her immediately.

'I'm not really in dire need of a nurse,' admitted the woman after Jancy had listed her qualifications and she in her turn had outlined the duties Jancy would undertake should she decide to employ her, 'although I do have this heart trouble. I need a companion more than anything else. Would that bother you?'

Jancy shook her head, she would do anything to get away from Saxon Marriot.

'You'd have your own sitting room, of course, and there's no reason why you should not entertain your friends. I wouldn't expect you to be on duty twenty-four hours a day. Have you a boyfriend?'

Again Jancy shook her head. Too strongly, she feared a second later when Mrs Fairfax frowned anxiously. But all her prospective employer said was, 'Good! And how about family? Will your parents object to you taking a live-in job?'

'My parents are abroad—my father's in the Army, and my sister has her own flat.'

'So in fact this job will be ideal. You have no ties?'

'None,' agreed Jancy.

'Why do you want to leave the hospital? Most girls prefer company their own age. You might find it lonely.'

Jancy had expected this question. 'I wanted a change, Mrs Fairfax. I've always fancied private nursing but thought I was too young. I took a gamble when I answered your advertisement.'

'I like young blood around me,' admitted the woman, 'but I want to be sure you're moving for the right reasons, not because you're running away from—someone?'

Jancy realised Mrs Fairfax was more perceptive than she gave her credit for. 'I'll be honest with you,' she said after a moment's hesitation. 'There was someone, but it's all over. It was very one-sided and now he has no interest in me whatsoever.'

'I see. He works at the hospital, I presume, this boy? I hope you're not going to be lovesick. I couldn't stand that.'

'Oh, no!' Jancy's eyes were wide and positive. 'He made it quite clear he never wants to see me again—and I've accepted that. I just want to move so that I won't be forced into seeing him each day. It's very painful.'

'In that case you're making a wise choice,'

nodded the woman. 'Staying at the General would simply add to your heartache. You're a sensible girl, I can see that, and I'm sure you won't let it affect your work. The job's yours if you want it?'

The money she offered was ridiculous under the circumstances and Jancy knew she would be a fool to turn it down, even though it seemed a waste of her qualifications.

She accepted enthusiastically and a week later moved into the Fairfax household—and met Giles! Giles was Mrs Fairfax's only son, in his mid-twenties, bright and breezy, tall and athletic. He was up each morning for a swim before going to work, played squash or went jogging most evenings. But for all that he was entertaining company on the occasions that Jancy had anything to do with him.

So far as physique went there was nothing between him and Saxon. They were both tall, powerful and well built, but that was where the resemblance ended. Giles had a high broad forehead, open features and an engaging grin. He had a shock of sandy hair and was totally honest, sometimes blunt to the point of being rude. He was at his happiest when in a crowd.

In fact he was just the diversion Jancy needed. Mrs Fairfax liked Jancy to join them for their evening meal, which the older woman always cooked herself, and Giles kept them both entertained with amusing stories of things that had happened during the day.

He worked for an advertising company in the city and judging by the stories he told Jancy decided he must enjoy his work very much. The people he worked with sounded a happy lot.

He had no particular girlfriend, although Jancy

learned from his mother that he had dated plenty. 'He's not yet ready to settle down, the dear boy, and I can't really say I want him to. It's been pretty hard since my husband died. I don't know what I'd do without Giles.'

Jancy could not see Giles sitting at home with his mother night after night. He was not the sort of man who could keep still for long. Even watching television he grew restless.

The first time he invited Jancy to go jogging she refused, believing his mother would object. She was after all an employee, not a friend of the family. But when Mrs Fairfax heard she insisted that Jancy join him whenever she liked.

And so Jancy began a new way of life. Giles was fun to be with and did not seem to be after a physical relationship for which Jancy was grateful. If Giles wanted her to be his friend then she was fully prepared to be that—but no more.

Inevitably she still thought about Saxon, but discovered she could live without him, and as the days and weeks passed the pain lessened, although she knew it would always be there. It was impossible to love a man such as Saxon and then forget him.

But she should have known that Giles would not settle for a permanent platonic relationship. In fact she would not have thought much of him as a man if he had.

After a particularly energetic game of squash, when for once she had beaten him, she laughed into his face. 'It serves you right for being such a big head.'

'You mean I shouldn't have taught you so well?' He too was laughing, but his face changed as he pulled her roughly against him, and the next moment he was kissing her with an intenseness that was surprising.

Jancy did not pull away, nor did she find his kisses unpleasant, although they held none of the fire that set her alive when Saxon kissed her. Her affair with Saxon had been a unique experience. She could not expect to find love like that again. Giles' advances were not distasteful, though, and given time she was sure she could get used to the idea of a deeper relationship.

When he set her back from him he was smiling. 'I've wanted to do that for a long time.'

'Then why haven't you?' she mocked, even though she was secretly relieved that he hadn't. If he had tried to kiss her in the early stages of their friendship she would most certainly have rejected him.

'Because you've always had an untouchable air. I've been frightened to approach you. Mother said you were getting over a broken romance. Is that right?'

She nodded and tried not to let her pain show.

'And you're over him now, this guy, whoever he was?'

Never would she be over him completely, but there was no point in hanging on to past memories. She was being given a chance to free herself, she must grab at it with both hands. 'Completely,' she smiled, 'and thank you for being patient.'

He grinned and gathered her to him again. 'How about another game of squash.'

'You're incorrigible,' retorted Jancy.

'I have no intention of letting a woman beat me,' he quipped.

'I already have.'

'That's what I mean. I must even things up.'

The game was swift and energetic and by the end of it Jancy collapsed, conceding that he was the best player and that, yes, it had been a fluke that she had won earlier.

Mrs Fairfax was delighted to see how well they were getting on, and Jancy suspected her employer entertained the idea that a deeper relationship might develop. It was premature of the woman to think this, but nevertheless it did not give Jancy any cause for concern. Giles was a super guy, full of fun, never serious for long, never allowing her to get down in the doldrums.

She doubted he would ever pay her compliments like Saxon had. Saxon really knew how to treat a woman, how to make her feel precious and feminine and desirable. Giles on the other hand wanted a partner, a friend, someone to join in his pursuit of physical fitness. She had no doubt he wanted a good lover too, but that was all in the future. She was glad he had not pressed home his advantage, she preferred a relationship that was not cluttered with physical emotions.

But gradually over the weeks their friendship deepened. It was a regular thing now for him to kiss her and never once did she hurt his feelings by rejecting him, even though she could not give him the response she had once given Saxon.

She felt guilty because of it and began to wonder what it would be like married to Giles, deciding it would not be a bad thing after all. Not that he had got so far as asking her to marry him, but he treated her as though she was going to be around for a long time.

And then one day Mrs Fairfax announced that she and Giles were going on a cruise and that she would like Jancy to accompany them. 'In your official capacity, of course,' she smiled.

'I couldn't,' said Jancy at once. 'I'd feel a fraud. I do already, as a matter of fact. There's hardly anything for me to do. You'll be well looked after on your voyage, you really won't need me. It would be wasting your money.'

'What else am I expected to do with it?' Mrs Fairfax was adamant. 'My husband died a wealthy man, not that his money did him much good. I intend spending it.'

After that Jancy could not wait for the day to arrive. It would be a once in a lifetime experience. She perused the brochures Mrs Fairfax had obtained. Two weeks in the Caribbean! It would be bliss.

The flight from Heathrow to Miami was exhilarating enough, in spite of its length, but the excitement when they sailed was the headiest thing Jancy had experienced—outside her relationship with Saxon, of course. Listening to the brass band playing on the quayside, throwing streamers to the waving crowd, were moments she would remember for a long time.

Seeing the Florida coast slowly fade into the distance, the strains of *We are Sailing* following them out to sea, made her feel that she was beginning a new life, even though she knew she would be coming back in all too short a space of time.

She could pretend, though. Pretend that at last she was rid of Saxon, rid of all thoughts of him. Six months had passed. She was free of him now, out here on the shiny blue ocean. There was just her and Giles. They would have fun. She would enjoy herself. If Saxon could not accept that she was telling him the truth then he did not deserve a place in her heart.

The *Ocean Queen* was like a vast floating hotel, even more impressive than it had looked in the brochure. At first Jancy was sure she would never find her way around its eight decks, pleasantly surprised how quickly she got used to it.

She counted eleven public rooms, four bars and three dance floors, as well as a theatre, card room and library. There were shops, beauty salons, swimming pools. Every possible need of the holidaymaker was catered for.

Jancy admired the relaxed and carefree attitude of their fellow cruisers, and after even just a few hours out at sea really did begin to feel she was getting Saxon out of her system. She and Giles were constant companions that day, playing deck tennis and quoits, swimming, jogging, and sunbathing.

She was the best friend any man could have, he said to her on their first evening on board. It was a typical Giles statement. Not for him the softly whispered words of love, although she was sure his feelings went as deep as anyone else's.

But the next morning on their first full day at sea, Mrs Fairfax announced she was not feeling well and wanted the ship's doctor to give her a check over. Jancy rang for him immediately and received the biggest shock of her life when she opened their cabin door a few minutes later.

Nothing had prepared her for this moment. Saxon Marriot was the last man she expected to see. The last man she wanted to see! She looked at him as though he were a ghost, the colour draining from her face, her throat becoming tinder-dry. He belonged to her past. He had no right walking back into her life.

Saxon on the other hand did not seem at all surprised to see her, and she guessed he already knew of her presence. His blue eyes slid over her, taking in the long length of leg exposed by her brief denim shorts, her trim waist and the sudden rise and fall of her pert breasts beneath the thin cotton T-shirt, lingering on the pulse racing erratically at the base of her throat, before finally locking his gaze into hers.

It was as electrifying now as it had been on that day of Kate's party. His eyes were as blue as she remembered, the outer navy ring emphasising the ultra-white whites, his thick lashes forming a sooty frame around them. They were narrowed slightly as if he was trying to assess her reaction to his unexpected presence.

She could do no more than shake her head and stand back for him to enter. After a brief, tension-filled second he moved past her, making his way towards the bed where Mrs Fairfax lay.

As he spoke in low tones to her employer Jancy could not take her eyes off him. His white shirt outlined the breadth of shoulder, the powerful chest. His black trousers moulded his still-slim hips and hard flat stomach. He had not changed at all. He was still a volatile, sexy, male animal—and she wished her heart would stop hammering!

She wondered what had made him give up his job at the General. It was a damning coincidence that they should meet again like this. It was the last place she had expected to see him. All her old emotions came tumbling to the surface and she realised painfully that she still loved him as much as ever—despite the way he had treated her!

His consultation with the older woman over, Saxon straightened and looked directly at Jancy.

She had forgotten quite how tall he was. He dwarfed the cabin, made it difficult to breathe, and she drew in a great gulp of air before turning so that their eyes should not meet.

He reached the door in a couple of strides and too late Jancy wished she had moved. He was so close she could smell the tangy aftershave that was his trademark, feel the warmth of his body even though several inches separated them.

'I'd like a word with you later.' His voice was a low husky growl and it sent shivers down her spine. But no way was she going to let him see that he still affected her. He had chosen to end their relationship. She would go along with that, whatever the cost.

'Not if I can help it,' she hissed. 'If I never see you again until my dying day it will be once too often.' Her green eyes flashed and the deep copper of her hair glowed with an inner fire. She tossed her head and pushed past him towards her employer who was watching them with a curious expression in her pale blue eyes. The door closed with a resounding bang.

'What a dishy young man.' Mrs Fairfax smiled encouragingly at Jancy. 'Makes me wish I was thirty years younger. I hope you introduced yourself? I couldn't quite catch what you were saying.'

'Mr Marriot and I have met before,' informed Jancy quietly.

'I see. What a coincidence. Did you work together?'

Jancy nodded, hoping the woman wouldn't realise that this was the man she had been running away from.

When Giles popped his head round the door

Jancy welcomed the diversion. 'I thought I'd take Jancy off for a swim, if you don't need her, Mother?' Then he realised that his parent was still in bed. He frowned and came further into the room. 'Are you ill? You both look very serious. Is something wrong?'

'Nothing,' said his mother immediately. 'I felt a bit weary, that's all, and called the doctor. But I'm fine. He simply told me to take things easy.'

'Are you sure?' Giles looked uncomfortable. Jancy had already discovered that he never seemed to know what to do where illness was concerned. It embarrassed him—which was probably why Mrs Fairfax had engaged a nurse.

'Perfectly,' announced the woman. 'Take Jancy by all means. There's nothing more she can do. I'm going to spend the morning in bed.'

Looking at Giles as he spoke to his mother the difference between him and Saxon struck Jancy more forcibly than it had at any other time. Saxon was a strong, dominant male who had taken over her life completely. Such was the power of his personality that when he walked into a room it was as though a charge of dynamite had been ignited. During the period of their relationship he had filled her every waking thought, demanding and getting total response. She had been his to do with as he liked, adoring him, loving him, wanting to spend the rest of her life with him.

Giles, on the other hand, never forced himself on her, never demanded more than she was prepared to give. He was considerate and a lot of fun. She had never had one sad moment since meeting him. He did not have Saxon's startling good looks. No woman would turn her head to take a second glance, but he was cheerful and friendly, and easy to get on with. There were never any complications in her life with Giles. No ups and downs. It went along at an even keel and she knew that if ever he did ask her to marry him her future would be safe and secure. Surely that counted for more than anything else?

She smiled warmly at Giles now. His sandy hair was blown into disarray, his body dewed with perspiration. Brief white shorts revealed tanned athletic legs. He had already been jogging along the promenades and open decks of the *Ocean Queen*. It was a wonder he had not asked her to join him. The thought of a swim now was welcome. She was hot and sticky and needed some positive action to rid Saxon Marriot from her mind.

But still Giles hesitated.

'Run along,' urged his mother. 'If I need Jancy I'll send the cabin steward for her. You two enjoy yourselves. That's what this cruise is all about.'

'It's for your benefit, Mrs Fairfax, you know that,' protested Jancy at once. 'I'm here to work, not play. I leave you alone far too much.'

'At the moment there is nothing you can do.' Mrs Fairfax's blue eyes twinkled as she pushed her hair back with an impatient hand. 'Except perhaps telephone the hair salon, book me an appointment for later this afternoon. My hair's such a mess.'

Jancy smiled inwardly. Mrs Fairfax's hair was never a mess. It was styled and permed regularly. She spent as much money on her appearance in one week as many women did in a whole year.

For the rest of the day Jancy was on tenterhooks, desperately afraid she might bump into Saxon again, relieved when she saw nothing of him.

Mrs Fairfax had overcome her lethargy and was as bright and cheerful as ever, suggesting after dinner that Jancy go with Giles to the excellent cabaret, or simply dance the night away.

But Jancy was in no mood for any of this. The whole atmosphere of this cruise had been spoiled by the chance appearance of Saxon Marriot. She knew that for the rest of the voyage she would be unable to relax.

Once she had settled Mrs Fairfax she went to bed herself. The settee in the adjoining sitting room converted into a bed and Mrs Fairfax had suggested that Jancy sleep here rather than in a separate cabin.

Giles had his own single cabin on the opposite side of the corridor, but as Jancy settled into bed she knew his room was empty. He had been displeased when she refused to join him. 'Some fun this trip's going to be if you go to bed early every night,' he said crossly.

'I'm sorry,' said Jancy. 'I have a headache.'

He looked at her disbelievingly. 'You've been different today. Something's happened, hasn't it? You're a bit like the girl who first came to our house.'

Jancy should have known she would be unable to hide her feelings, but she could not tell him that her past lover was on board. That would be disastrous. More than likely Giles would black Saxon's eyes, and that was the last thing she wanted.

'I really do have a headache,' she insisted. 'I'll be better tomorrow.'

With that he had to be satisfied.

The gentle movement of the ship, the distant throb of the engines, would normally have lulled Jancy to sleep. But tonight there was none of that.

Saxon Marriot had completely destroyed her peace of mind.

When Mrs Fairfax looked at Jancy the next morning she demanded to know whether she was ill. 'I've never seen you so pale and washed out. What on earth is the matter?'

'I couldn't sleep,' said Jancy. 'It must be the heat.' Which was a poor excuse if ever there was one, as Mrs Fairfax must know, because all of the cabins were individually air-conditioned.

'Then it's a lazy day for you,' said her employer firmly. 'It's your turn to rest today. You can have your breakfast on deck and then lie on one of the loungers until lunch time.'

Jancy dared not argue, but knew that doing nothing was not the answer. It would give her too much time for thought. She opened the door to their cabin steward who brought in Mrs. Fairfax's early morning cup of tea, remaining silent until he had gone, then she said, 'I might join Giles for a game of deck tennis. He was so disappointed when I went to bed early last night. He likes me to be with him.'

Mrs Fairfax frowned. 'Don't overdo it. I know what he's like. He'll run you into the ground if you're not careful.'

Jancy laughed. 'Who's the nurse here? I thought I was supposed to be looking after you.'

'I don't need a nurse, as you well know,' smiled her employer. 'Play tennis if you like, but take it easy. It's much hotter here than it was in England. It's bound to take it out of you.'

Giles came to their cabin then in a pair of pale blue shorts and a white vest. Again he had taken his early morning run. The sight of so much energy made Jancy feel even more tired.

'Morning, Mother. Morning, Jancy,' he said cheerfully.

Jancy smiled weakly and Mrs Fairfax said, 'I want you to look after Jancy today, Giles. She's feeling fragile. See that she gets plenty of rest.'

He frowned. 'You're not sick, are you?' He could not stand weakness in a person. He seemed to think they should all be as disgustingly fit as himself. 'How's your head?'

'Better,' said Jancy quickly. 'I didn't sleep too well, that's all. Your mother's exaggerating.'

'Nevertheless,' said the older woman firmly, 'it won't hurt you to pamper yourself. You run around after me far too much, and trying to keep up with Giles cannot possibly be good for you.'

So Jancy took her breakfast on the open deck near the swimming pool. As with all the meals served on the *Ocean Queen* the choice was staggering. The long buffet table groaned beneath the weight of huge bowls of cereal. There was fresh fruit galore, including succulent pineapple, green figs and prunes. Jugs of chilled fruit juice stood side by side with croissants, muffins, and all sorts of bread.

And if something hot was preferred there were grilled kippers, poached Finnan Haddock, eggs done in any number of ways. Bacon, sausages, minute steaks, kidneys. Everything you could think of.

Jancy settled for a glass of orange and a roll but Giles tucked into a bowl of cereal followed by a mammoth cooked breakfast, washing it down with several cups of tea.

Afterwards Jancy lay on one of the gaily striped loungers. If the truth were known it felt good to be doing absolutely nothing, enjoying the brilliant sunshine, listening to the cries of the children in the pool, the snatches of conversation around her. Keeping up with Giles was enervating. This was supposed to be a holiday, not a marathon. His energy was inexhaustible. He could not sit still for more than a few minutes at a time.

Later she played a couple of games of tennis with him, spent a little time standing at the ship's rail watching another vessel far away, but most of the morning she drowsed under the soporific rays of the sun, staying where there were plenty of people, where she could be sure of not bumping into Saxon Marriot.

When she returned to their cabin just before lunch she was surprised to see how cheerful Mrs Fairfax looked. 'Something nice happened?' she asked, laughing. 'You look like a cat who's stolen the cream.'

'I had a visitor,' announced the older woman with satisfaction.

'Someone who's done you good by the look of it.'

Her employer nodded. 'That dishy young surgeon. He came to see how I was. Wasn't that kind of him?'

Jancy blanched. 'Very,' she commented drily, wondering whether it had been herself he was looking for. He had said he wanted to talk. Though as far as she was concerned there was nothing to say. There was no point in resurrecting old memories—especially painful ones.

'We had a long discussion,' said Mrs Fairfax. 'He was surprised to hear you were my nurse. He thought you were Giles' girlfriend. I told him you were that as well, of course.'

Good for you, thought Jancy. That would show him. He would know she was not pining for him.

'He said it was a pity you'd left the hospital, that you were a very good nurse.'

Jancy's eyes widened, but before she could respond Mrs Fairfax continued, 'But the best news is that he's suggested we sit at his table. Won't that be exciting? I bet he has a few tales to tell.'

Jancy was horrified. This was the last thing she wanted. Why on earth had he arranged for them to do that? What possible good could it do?

This whole cruise was fast becoming a nightmare.

CHAPTER THREE

IT was with trepidation that Jancy dressed for lunch, not that she expected Saxon to be in the restaurant at that time of day. He would be far too busy. Nevertheless it was nerve-racking walking into the elegant room, her relief knowing no bounds when he was missing.

But she hardly touched her meal. Mrs Fairfax on the other hand ate heartily, which was unusual in itself. All Jancy could do was push her food about her plate and hope no one would notice.

But Giles saw and said rawly, 'I hope you're not sickening for something, Jancy?' His normally cheerful features were disfigured with a scowl.

'I'm fine,' she answered, endeavouring to pull herself together. This wouldn't do, not at all. With an effort she chewed and swallowed, even though the gammon tasted like sawdust, the accompanying sauce like quinine. She had never felt less like eating in her life.

She managed to enter into conversation with a blonde woman who introduced herself as Debra Forrester, though even this was a mistake when it transpired that she had fallen under the spell of the ship's surgeon.

'Isn't he the most gorgeous man you've ever set eyes on?' she asked. 'I don't know who was responsible for the seating arrangements but I couldn't have fixed it better myself. Lucky you, being moved to his table. Have you met him yet? If not you're in for a treat.'

'Oh, yes,' said Jancy coolly, 'but I'm afraid I don't share your opinion.'

'Is that so?' Debra Forrester arched her finely pencilled brows. 'My husband never looks at me the way he does. I think I'm going to enjoy this cruise after all.'

The woman chattered on in the same vein throughout the entire meal and Jancy was glad when it was over. Except that dinner still loomed ahead and Saxon would surely be present then. She wondered whether she could plead yet another headache?

However, her meeting with Saxon came long before dinner. Mrs Fairfax joined the bridge game in the card room only to discover she had left her glasses behind. 'Fetch them for me, Jancy, there's a dear.'

When a tap came on the cabin door as she was searching for them Jancy assumed it to be the cabin steward and smiled readily. Discovering Saxon confronting her wiped the smile from her face. 'I'm sorry, Mrs Fairfax isn't here.' Her tone was barely civil, though her heart leapt violently.

His lips firmed, but he said equably. 'It's not her I've come to see, it's you. We must talk.' He pushed her to one side and strode into the cabin, shutting the door firmly behind him.

With no compunction he propelled her towards the settee, pushing her roughly down on to it. Turning towards the drinks cupboard he poured a measure of whisky.

Jancy watched him as she had so many times in the past, her heart as full of love as ever it had been. But there was no way she was going to let Saxon see this. He had hurt her, he had wounded her pride, and it would be a long time, if ever, before she forgave him.

He handed her the drink, his piercing blue eyes never once leaving her face. 'Strictly for medicinal purposes. You look as though you need it.'

'I don't want it—and I don't want to talk to you.' Jancy was angry, her green eyes flashing fire. 'I'm over you now. In fact I would go so far as to say that you did me a good turn by finishing our affair.'

Pain flickered through his eyes and she realised that he was thinner, deep lines were etched in the shadows of his face, silver hairs streaking the glossy black.

'Are you in love with Giles Fairfax?' His voice was harsh, rasping in the air, filling the cabin with tension.

Jancy lifted her chin and stared strongly. 'I don't see that it's any concern of yours.'

'And Mrs Fairfax,' he continued crisply, 'I'm quite sure she doesn't need a private nurse. I wonder how you managed to persuade her?' His lips curled contemptuously.

Jancy flicked him a cold look. 'The job was advertised. I'm also well aware that she doesn't need me, but the money she offered was——'

'The money?' he cut in cruelly, making Jancy realise she had made a mistake mentioning it. 'Does she realise she's paying you for her son's services?'

'How dare you!' Jancy was incensed, standing up and swinging her arm in an arc, her palm flattened, aiming straight for his face. But this time he was quicker than she, gripping her wrist, stopping her in mid-air, pulling her mercilessly against him.

She felt the erratic thump of his heart, the

tension of his limbs, the heat of his body. 'God, I hate you, Saxon Marriot. You have a disgusting mind. If you're really interested I'm going to marry Giles. Do you hear? Marry him! He's a far better man than you!'

It was a profound statement considering Giles had never asked her, but at that moment Jancy was prepared to lie as much as she need to get him out of her cabin. It sickened her to realise that he thought she was offering her body to Giles in the same manner as he had accused her of doing to him.

And then as suddenly as he had pulled her against him he let her go. 'I don't see why you're going to the trouble of marrying him when you're obviously getting what you want. I've seen the two of you together. He never takes his eyes off you for one moment. You've certainly got him eating out of your hand.'

The ocean green of Jancy's eyes flashed dangerously. 'Giles is not like that. He's good and kind and never, ever, takes advantage.'

'I doubt he'd need to,' flung Saxon coldly. 'If you're the same with him as you were with me he'd certainly need no encouraging.'

Jancy stamped her foot indignantly. 'Get out! Get out of here now! I refuse to be insulted by you for one moment longer.'

She crossed towards the door but he stood in her way, fixing his big hands on her shoulders. His sinister smile should have warned her, but she was shaking with an anger more intense than anything she had felt in her life and was blind to his intentions.

'I think,' he said, his soft voice far more menacing, 'that we ought to carry out an experiment.' He pulled her towards him, determination in his eyes.

Jancy struggled ineffectually against his superior strength. 'Leave me alone,' she grated. 'You cannot do this, I will not let you.'

He grinned maliciously. 'Stop me if you can.'

As their bodies met a charge of electricity ran through Jancy's limbs. This was the one thing that would let her down, crack the defensive shell she had built around herself. She fixed her eyes on his as his head came closer, seeing the confidence, hating it, but unable to ignore the painful beat of her heart. She was throbbingly, vibrantly, alive—and he had not yet kissed her! What was it about this man that made her still love him when he treated her like dirt?

Standing as still and cold as a statue when his mouth captured hers was the hardest thing she had ever done, but she refused to give in, not even allowing herself one moment of pleasure. She had to be strong. He had treated her abominably and did not deserve the merest flicker of response.

When it became evident he was getting nowhere Saxon put her from him. She dared to glance up and was pleased to see the tight anger on his face, the hurt, the disappointment. 'You see,' she said triumphantly, 'it's all over. You no longer mean anything to me.'

He shook his head. 'Nothing will ever convince me of that. You're playing a part. You turned to Giles for comfort and I freely admit it was my fault.'

'What are you trying to say?' she asked tightly.

'That I'd like to resume our—er, relationship.' His voice was tense and hard, but oddly pleading too.

Jancy looked at him incredulously. 'You have a nerve. Twice you've wrongly accused me. I'm certainly not giving you the opportunity of doing it a third time. Whatever we had going for us, Saxon, is over and done with. My employer tells me you've arranged for us to sit at your table. I'd be obliged if you'd cancel those arrangements.'

Saxon's nostrils flared, his lips grew white. 'You really do hate me, don't you, Jancy?'

Jancy's triumph was tinged with sadness. 'What made you think I'd come running into your arms again?'

'I never thought it would be easy,' he said, 'but I hoped you'd at least listen. I've been trying to find you.'

'Really?' Her heart stopped and then hammered against her rib-cage. But there was no change in her expression. She was as cold and distant as it was possible to be. 'I can't think why. You wouldn't listen to me.'

'I made a big mistake,' he said. 'I've been talking to your friend, Ruth. I discovered you were telling the truth after all.'

This did shock Jancy but still she eyed him coldly. 'And you think that apologising will make it better? Not that I altogether believe you. You could have found me if you'd really wanted to. Ruth knew where I was.'

'Ruth wouldn't tell me,' he said sadly. 'She said you didn't want anything more to do with me— ever.'

'Nor do I,' snapped Jancy. 'You've completely ruined my holiday. I was enjoying it until you turned up. What made you leave the hospital?'

'My job there was never permanent,' he said, 'but it's not me we're discussing.'

'And it's certainly not me.' Jancy eyed him belligerently. 'Okay, so you now know I was telling the truth, but that doesn't alter the fact that you doubted me, thought the worst of me. Do you think I'd ever be able to trust you again? All the time I'd wonder whether you believed what I said, whether you suspected the motives behind anything I did. It's not the sort of life I want, Saxon. Giles and I have a very good relationship and I'd thank you not to ruin it. Now, if you don't mind, I really must go. Mrs Fairfax will wonder where I am.'

She snatched up her employer's glasses and this time he made no attempt to detain her. He was surprisingly calm, appearing to have accepted the situation, though Jancy knew him better than that. This was the calm before the storm. He would not give up so easily.

While sitting in the card room, absently gazing out of the long windows at the shiny deep blue ocean Jancy went over their conversation. Saxon really had a nerve thinking she would return to him after all that had happened. Didn't he realise that hurting a girl's pride was the worst thing he could do?

No matter that she still loved him it would never work. Always at the back of Saxon's mind would be the memory of the way she had offered herself to him on that first meeting. He might regret his outburst, declare that he'd made a big mistake, but deep down he would always wonder. And it would not take much to trigger off his suspicions again. It was a risk she was unwilling to take. Oh, why had he turned up just when she was beginning to get over him?

When the bridge game had finished Jancy accompanied Mrs Fairfax to the Sun Deck where they lay and enjoyed the warm late-afternoon sunshine. But all too soon it was time to get ready for dinner. Jancy dreaded it. Coming on top of her meeting with Saxon this afternoon it would be an even greater ordeal.

She showered and slipped into a cream dress in soft georgette. It was cut low with thin shoulder straps and superb flowing lines. It was one of many new dresses Mrs Fairfax had insisted she buy, footing the bill herself much to Jancy's embarrassment. It had its own scarf which she arranged carefully about her neck, pinning gold hoops to her ears and a matching bracelet to her wrist.

She had brushed her hair until it shone like burnished copper, looping back the sides only, leaving the rest to fall about her shoulders in a silken curtain, adding more make-up than usual to her pale face.

They joined the other passengers in the Columbine Bar for cocktails, Mrs Fairfax deciding to try a Harvey Wallbanger, Jancy settling for a dry sherry.

Her employer was soon lost in conversation with another couple and Jancy and Giles were left to themselves. 'I hope you're enjoying this cruise, Jancy,' he said sharply. 'You're not yourself today, even now I can tell your smile's artificial. I wish you'd tell me what's wrong. You look like you've lost every penny you possess.'

Jancy wondered whether she dared admit the truth—but decided against it. It could cause a great deal of unpleasantness and she wanted to avoid that at all costs. 'There really is nothing wrong,' she said irritably. 'Can't a girl have an off day without an inquisition?'

His brows rose at the sharpness of her tone. 'I'm merely thinking of you, Jancy. There is something wrong and there's no point in denying it. I just hope you're not going to let whatever it is spoil our holiday. Drink up, I'll get you something stronger.'

He returned with a glass of golden liquid topped with a slice of orange and a cherry. Jancy took a sip and looked at him questioningly. It tasted pretty potent.

'Brandy Crusta,' he informed. 'Cognac and orange curaçao, with a dash of lemon juice, maraschino and angostura. I trust you like it?'

'It's very strong,' admitted Jancy, 'but quite nice.' Indeed it had a most warming effect and by the time she got to the bottom of the glass she felt she could handle whatever the evening held in store.

Her cheeks glowed and when the dinner chimes sounded and they made their way below to the Kasbah Restaurant she held Giles' hand tightly.

It was a most beautiful room; concealed lighting enhancing the timber-clad walls, the carpeting a deep soft turquoise. There were silk wall hangings and cases of exquisite porcelain. The tables were dressed in brilliant white with gleaming silver and glass. Nowhere in the world would you have found a more stylish restaurant.

Saxon was already at his table and Jancy wondered how she had missed him on other nights they dined here. He stood out from those around him; even the captain was not such an imposing figure. His white dinner jacket emphasised his depth of tan, the breadth of shoulder, and before she was anywhere near him his eyes found hers. She was conscious of him watching her progress across the room. They could have been the only

two people present. Everyone else faded into
oblivion as she felt the magnetic pull of this man.

Much to her horror he stood up as they
approached, seating her next to him, Mrs Fairfax
on his other side. There was to be no escape. She
could only hope that her employer would
monopolise his attention throughout the meal.

Yet even that seemed doubtful, because sitting
next to Mrs Fairfax was a gentleman much older
than Saxon. A fine figure of a man nevertheless,
with a snowy white beard and a good head of hair.
He looked intelligent and his twinkling eyes
suggested a keen sense of humour. Jancy had no
doubt that he would keep Mrs Fairfax admirably
entertained.

Indeed, already he was looking at her in
appreciation. Despite the fact that she was nearing
sixty Mrs Fairfax had a good figure still, and her
hair, expertly arranged by one of the ship's very
good hairdressers, was stylishly elegant. Her
fingers were heavy with diamonds and sapphires,
her carefully manicured nails pastel pink, and her
blue eyes shone as they rested on the stranger.

Jancy's spirits dropped and it did not help
matters to discover that the remaining vacant seat
was beside Debra Forrester and Giles had been
forced to take it. The gentleman on her own other
side looked as though he had eyes for no one
except his attractive partner. Saxon had arranged
it all very neatly.

Her warm glow faded and she listened uninterestedly as Saxon introduced the other
members of the table. Mrs Fairfax's jolly
gentleman was a retired admiral, Jacob Honeydew.
Debra Forrester was the wife of a bank manager
holidaying alone to get over a recent illness. The

gentleman next to Jancy, David Nelson, was the president of some giant American corporation, and the girl with him was the widow of a well-known racing driver tragically killed last year.

Jancy wished she had insisted on wearing her uniform on this cruise, then she would never have been invited to sit at the surgeon's table. It was an ordeal already. How was she going to get through the rest of the holiday?

'You've lost weight.' Saxon's eyes were upon her, his voice critical, with none of the soft undertones that had once melted her bones.

'It's fashionable to be slim,' she said distantly.

'But not painfully thin,' came the quick response. 'Has it anything to do with me? Your friend, Ruth, told me you were pretty cut up about some of the things I said.'

'Don't flatter yourself,' crisped Jancy, feeling that he was stripping her naked, that he was seeing through the flimsy material of her dress to her body that was so much thinner. Damn Ruth for telling him how upset she had been. She made a pretence of studying the menu.

'At least the food's good here,' he said, 'and with the sea air you should soon fatten out. I shall look for an improvement by the end of the voyage.'

'Are you speaking as a doctor or a friend?' she snapped. 'Why should it matter to you what I look like?'

'I'd like to think it's both,' he said, and then adroitly changed the subject. 'Why have you thrown all your years of training away?'

She tossed her head angrily. 'I wanted a change.'

'I'd have thought more of you if you'd stayed. Running away made you look guilty.'

'In that case I can't think why you bothered to find out the truth,' she retorted. Only she saw the grim lines about his mouth. The next moment the waiter enquired whether she was ready to order and it was good to turn her attention to something else.

It was difficult to make her choice from the very extensive selection on the menu. In the end she ordered green pea soup and grilled salmon fillet, but was quite sure that with Saxon at her side she would be unable to eat.

'I suggest,' said Saxon smoothly, 'that you forget I'm out of favour for the moment. We're getting some funny looks.'

'You mean,' commented Jancy drily, 'that I'm to fall all over you, like every other woman here? Like I did once, fool that I was?' There was fire in her eyes as she looked into his face. 'I hate you, Saxon Marriot, so it's no use asking me to pretend. You'd be doing both yourself and me a favour if you'd change the seating arrangements.'

His nostrils flared. 'I take it you're not prepared to meet me even half way?'

She shook her head. 'Not an inch of the way. You hurt me like no one has ever done before. You stripped me into shreds and Giles put me back together. So far as I'm concerned you no longer exist, is that clear?'

She had been ready for his anger, but was unprepared when he pushed back his chair and stood up. 'Excuse me, ladies and gentlemen. I've just been given a sign that I'm needed in the hospital. Enjoy your meal.'

He did not look at her again but his coat sleeve brushed her arm as he strode past and she shivered involuntarily. She could smell him. He had a

distinct scent all of its own and it lingered with her
long after he had gone. She had not expected to
hurt him so much that he had to make an excuse
to leave, but was glad she had done so. He
deserved it.

'The poor man,' said Debra Forrester brightly.
'One of the drawbacks of the job. Perhaps we'll see
him later?' Her eyes followed him as he weaved his
way through the sea of faces and Jancy noticed
that they were not the only ones to be attracted by
this magnetic man. Most of the women glanced
hungrily at him as he passed their table and Jancy
knew she was envied her seat next to him. What
fools they were. She would willingly have changed
with any one of them.

For the rest of the evening and the next morning
Jancy saw nothing more of Saxon. It should have
been a relief, was in fact the reverse. She was
unable to relax for more than two minutes at a
time, always on her guard in case he appeared. It
was ridiculous when there was so much entertainment on the ship, enough to keep her occupied
for every minute of the day if she desired, yet she
couldn't recapture that free and easy feeling.

She spent all of her time with Giles, when she
was not needed by Mrs Fairfax, joining in the energetic games he loved during the day, dancing that
evening, making sure he was constantly at her side.

He was pleased she had apparently got over her
bad patch. 'I thought this trip was going to be a
disaster,' he said, holding her comfortably against
him as they looked over the ship's rail.

In the far distance Jancy spotted Haiti and the
Dominican Republic, nothing more than a purple
mound on the horizon. How she wished she was
there instead of imprisoned on this ship, fearing

with every step she took that she might bump into Saxon Marriot.

She dragged her gaze back to Giles. 'This is a holiday of a lifetime,' she said brightly. 'I'd be pretty stupid to let anything spoil it.' Or anyone, she added to herself.

He kissed her warmly. 'I'm glad to hear it.'

Jancy tried to respond with some fervour, but sadly realised that her feelings for Giles were slowly dwindling. She could no longer feel pleasure in his kisses. They had never had half the power of Saxon's—he had never been able to cause that turmoil of emotion that sometimes drove her crazy—but she had always felt a mild sort of enjoyment and had thought that would do—up till now. Thankfully Giles seemed not to find anything wrong.

They used the indoor pool, alternating their swimming with bursts of energy on the exercise bikes and rowing equipment. Jancy then used the sauna; not really enjoying the heat, there was enough of that outside, but here was one place where she could be sure of not meeting Saxon.

That was until late in the afternoon a girl collapsed. There were only the two of them in the sauna and Jancy managed to drag her out and lie her on the tiles beside the pool. After a brief check she decided it was nothing more than the heat that had affected this young woman. Indeed her eyelids flickered seconds only after she had carried her out. But someone had already summoned the doctor.

It was Jancy's bad luck that it was Saxon himself who attended. She was kneeling beside the girl when he crouched down beside her, his eyes shooting from her to the prostrate form. 'What happened?'

'She passed out in the sauna.' Jancy's reply was as professional as she could make it.

The girl gave a weak self-conscious smile. 'It was stupid of me, I shouldn't have gone in there. I'm pregnant, you see, and not feeling too good at the moment.'

She certainly did not look pregnant, thought Jancy; the other woman's stomach being perfectly flat and smooth. Saxon swung his patient up into his arms as effortlessly as if she were a child. 'I think I'd better take you to the hospital and give you a check up, just to be on the safe side. Jancy, you come too.'

She snapped her eyes wide. 'What can I do?'

'You were on the scene when it happened. I might need some questions answering.'

Some excuse, she thought. Nevertheless, she followed, her feet dragging, her towel clutched tightly about her. The hospital was on the same deck so it took them no more than a few seconds to reach it.

Saxon lay the girl on the couch in his consulting room, carrying out a routine examination. 'Would you like me to send for your husband?'

The girl's eyes were fixed on the surgeon's face and Jancy could almost read the thoughts going through her head. It was the same with any woman who met him. They became intoxicated with the blueness of his eyes, his all-encompassing smile.

The girl shook her head. 'He's trying his luck at the tables. Besides, he'd only worry. I feel all right now, really I do.' She struggled to sit up. 'It took a long time to persuade him I was well enough to come on this cruise. We'd booked it, you see, before I was pregnant.'

'There should be no problem,' said Saxon, 'so long as you're sensible. No more overdoing it in the sauna, eh?'

The girl smiled weakly and Jancy felt sickened by the absolute trust on her face. Was that how she had once looked at him? She turned abruptly and fled from the room, ignoring his sharp, 'Jancy, wait!'

In her cabin she replaced her bikini with shorts and a strapless top, looking despairingly in the mirror at the lines of strain on her face. 'Damn you, Saxon Marriot,' she said out loud. 'How dare you come back into my life?'

As Giles seemed to have disappeared she scanned the daily news sheet to see what was going on and decided to attend the port talk in the theatre. Tomorrow they called at San Juan. It would be a welcome break to get off the ship and she wanted to find out as much as she could about Puerto Rico before they went ashore.

Mrs Fairfax had already declared that she intended going on the organised excursion with Jacob Honeydew. 'It won't be necessary for you to come with us,' she said. 'The admiral will look after me.'

Jancy smiled when told this. She was becoming more obsolete with each day that passed. Mrs Fairfax had been in the constant company of Admiral Honeydew since meeting him. In fact Jancy had never seen her in such high spirits. The admiral was certainly doing her good. And naturally Giles had asked Jancy to go with him. 'We'll hire a car,' he said, 'and go where we like.'

The talk in the theatre was extremely informative, but Jancy found it difficult to concentrate, and when she left was not a great deal wiser.

She learned that San Juan was the capital of Puerto Rico and that the main industry was sugar, that the temperature was pretty constant the whole year round, but that was about all. She had the strongest feeling that she would never get Saxon Marriot out of her mind. He would haunt her until her dying day.

There was still an hour before she need think about preparing for dinner, and as Giles was playing yet another energetic game of deck tennis she lay down on one of the striped loungers on the imitation green lawn of the Sun Deck.

She had collected an Agatha Christie thriller from the library, but although her eyes skimmed the pages she took none of it in. Intermittently came announcements over the loudspeaker system, but it was something of a shock when she heard her own name.

Will Nurse Ullman, travelling with Mrs Fiona Fairfax, please come to the hospital.

Jancy was on her feet in a flash. Something had happened to her employer! Automatically she looked across at Giles, wondering if he had heard, wanting him to come with her. But he had gone. He must have finished his game while she was attempting to read her book.

As the Sun Deck was topside she took the amidships lift to B Deck. She felt as breathless as if she had been running by the time she burst into the hospital, cannoning into Saxon Marriot himself.

His strong arms steadied her but she pulled free and looked frantically around. 'Where is she? What's wrong?'

'Who?' Saxon's face was an innocent mask.

'Mrs Fairfax, of course.' Jancy looked at him

impatiently but it took a few seconds for her to realise that her employer was not here. 'Mrs Fairfax is not ill, is she?' she accused angrily. 'You've got me here under false pretences. It was just you wanting to see me.'

'Why did you rush away?' He did not look in the least concerned that he had deceived her. 'I wished to talk to you.'

'But I don't want to talk to you,' she rasped.

His eyes narrowed. 'I'm not sure you know what is best.'

'And I'm damn sure you don't.' She hurled herself at the door, wrenching it open and tearing along the corridor as though all the hounds in hell were after her.

But she had gone no more than a few yards when Saxon caught up, grasping her wrist, yanking her to a halt. He opened a door and hustled her inside, closing it quietly, then standing up against it to effectively bar her escape.

Alarm flickered as Jancy realised she was inside Saxon's own cabin. Too late she wished she had not run out of the hospital. At least there would have been a chance they might be interrupted, here there was none. She was completely at his mercy.

'You'll get no satisfaction,' she announced savagely, her green eyes flashing, her breasts rising and falling as she took deep breaths of air, not realising how attractive she looked with her heightened colour and the glare of anger in her eyes.

'You can't keep avoiding me,' he said softly.

'Who says I've been avoiding you? You've been absent from dinner these last few days. I would say it was the other way round.'

He gave her a disappointed look. 'You think I

stayed away deliberately? You should know me better than that, Jancy. I was working, otherwise nothing would have kept me away.'

'You're wasting your time,' she snapped. 'No matter how much smooth talking you do you will never persuade me to leave Giles.'

His lips tightened impatiently. 'He's the wrong man for you. You must know that.'

'I know nothing of the kind,' Jancy retorted. 'You were the one who was wrong for me. Giles has never hurt me like you did.'

'Neither have I seen you looking at Giles the way you looked at me. You might think you love him, Jancy, but your feelings are superficial.'

'Feelings!' she hissed. 'What do you know about feelings? You can pick up a girl and then crush her without even losing any sleep over it.'

He looked pained. 'Do you think I'd have bothered to find out the truth if I'd had no feelings for you?'

She tossed her head proudly. 'If you'd had any at all you'd never have made those degrading accusations.'

'Hell!' He swung away savagely. 'I can see I'm getting nowhere. Would you like a drink?'

Jancy nodded. Although she did not relish the idea of being held in his cabin a drink was more than welcome. Her mouth was dry, her tongue like a chamois. 'I could do with a lager, my throat's parched. You don't know how I worried when I thought Mrs Fairfax was ill.'

'I knew it was the one thing guaranteed to bring you down here.' He flicked open the well-stocked fridge and selected a couple of cans, pulling the rings and pouring the contents into two glasses.

Jancy tooks hers, careful not to let her fingers

brush his. She traced a pattern in the mist that formed on the outside of the glass and took a long drink of the chilled lager, then she turned away and glanced around the cabin.

It was fairly impersonal and could have belonged to anyone—except for the onyx table lighter which stood prominently on the bedside table! It had been her present to him, given as a token of her love. She was surprised he had kept it.

She spun round, her heart thudding erratically. 'Just why have you brought me here?'

He smiled humourlessly, having seen her eyes alight on the gift. 'Isn't it obvious?' His glass was held between long hard fingers but he made no attempt to drink the contents.

'So that you can persuade me I'm making a mess of my life?' She lifted her brows scornfully and took another long swallow of the ice-cold beer.

'That as well,' he said, 'but primarily I want us to be friends again. I'm still very—er, fond of you, Jancy.'

'Don't give me that eyewash,' she spat. 'If you'd loved me you wouldn't have doubted me. You might desire me, but that's about all.'

He looked surprisingly hurt. 'Is that what you think?'

'It's what I know.' She slammed her glass down and crossed to the door, wondering why he made no attempt to stop her. When it would not open she knew the reason.

'If you think it will make any difference keeping me a prisoner, you're mistaken.' She drew herself up to her full height, glaring like an outraged tiger.

'We reach Puerto Rico tomorrow,' he said quietly. 'Since Mrs Fairfax has found a new friend I don't think she'll be needing you. I'd like you to accompany me ashore.'

Her chin came up sharply. 'You're forgetting Giles. I've already arranged to go with him.'

Saxon's eyes narrowed. 'As if I could forget the man you're going to marry, but I'm sure I could give you a better time than he. I know the island, I've been there before. I know exactly which places to visit and which to avoid. I'd like you to come with me.'

'And I'd like you to go to hell,' she grated. 'Have you any idea what Giles would say if I accepted your invitation? He doesn't even know we've met before.'

'You mean you haven't told him about us?' He looked shocked.

She shook her head violently, copper hair flying. 'When one's trying to forget something one doesn't go around talking about it.'

His face hardened at the condemning tone in her voice and again there was that characteristic flare of his nostrils. He finished his lager, his movements jerky, setting the glass down beside hers, then snatching her into his arms.

'You'll never forget me,' he snarled, 'and that's a promise.'

Her lips were ground back against her teeth as he claimed her mouth savagely. The kiss went on and on, drugging her senses, her struggles futile against the strength of this man.

When at length he lifted his head she parted her lips to drink in desperately needed air. It was a mistake. He pounced again, his kiss deepening, his urgent tongue exploring her soft moistness. Jancy had the strangest feeling that she was back in the past, that there had never been any mis-understanding between them.

His kisses were arousing in her all the old
familiar feelings, desire spiralled from the bottom
of her stomach to lodge in her throat. She gave an
uncontrollable moan and arched herself closer.

Fire ran like quicksilver through her limbs as
her arms tightened around him, feeling the tense
muscle of his shoulders, sliding her hands upwards
to mingle with the wiry dark hair.

She could feel the hard pulsating strength of his
body, the heat of his ardour, and knew that he was
as moved as she herself. All coherent thought fled
as she drifted into the old almost forgotten world
of sheer sensualism.

At that moment she desired Saxon like never
before, pressing ever closer, feeling the hard length
of thigh against hers, the unsteady beat of his
heart. His hands moved to coax her thin strapless
top downwards, revealing her breasts in all their
naked glory, cupping them, teasing as only he
knew how until she was squirming in an agony of
delight.

How many times had he done this to her in the
past? How many times had she lain in his arms
letting him arouse her like no one had ever done
before? At times like that she always longed for
him to make love—and today was no exception.

She was shocked by the depth of her feelings,
the discovery that the love she had tried to banish
was as strong and febrile as ever. She wanted him
achingly, desperately. His mouth moved to nuzzle
the softness of her throat and Jancy's head rolled
back on her shoulders, her eyes tightly closed, her
lips parted. 'Oh, Saxon,' she cried, quite oblivious
to what she was saying. 'Why are you doing this to
me?'

'Because, my sweet love,' he said, 'we are meant

for each other. Don't you know that? I tried to forget you, but I couldn't—and now I've found you I'm never going to let you go.' His voice was gruff, his breath ragged in his throat.

With a groan he buried his head in the sweetly scented valley between her breasts, taking each rosy peak in turn into his mouth. Jancy felt as though she was going out of her mind and when he lifted her into his arms she linked her hands readily behind his neck, allowing him to carry her to his bed.

She lay there, breathing heavily, her heart like jungle drums in her ears, her body writhing and pulsating with unfulfilled desire. What would have happened had the telephone not rung she did not know.

He answered it briskly, nothing in his tone suggesting that he had been interrupted in the act of making love. Jancy sat up, tugging her sun top back into position, wondering how he could switch from one mood to another so easily.

'I'm sorry,' he said when he had finished, trailing his fingers across her cheek and pressing a swift kiss to her brow. 'I have to go.'

She turned away. 'Not half so sorry as me.' Her tones were crisp. She had come to her senses with a jolt. 'I must have been insane to let you do that.'

'Not insane,' he said softly, 'merely answering the dictates of your heart. Bear with me, Jancy, I shouldn't be long.'

'You mean you think I'll be here when you come back? To hell with that, Saxon, I'm going. This has altered nothing. I was a fool letting my sexual desires get the better of me, but I won't put myself in the same situation again. I'm not coming with you tomorrow, I'm going with Giles.' She was as much angry with herself as she was with him.

'I'm sorry you feel like that.' He straightened his shirt and fixed his tie, running a comb through his hair where her eager fingers had tousled it. 'I really thought I was making progress.'

'Progress be damned,' she cried. 'You tricked me!'

A muscle jerked in his jaw as he gave her one final disappointed look, his face pale beneath its tan, lips tight. 'I don't intend giving up, Jancy. Keep that in mind for when we next meet.'

CHAPTER FOUR

WHEN Saxon left Jancy sank back on to the bed, feeling as limp and washed out as a rag doll. What on earth had possessed her? She had behaved like the seductress he had once accused her of being, telling him in no uncertain terms that he still had the power to turn her on.

It was an unfortunate situation. He would never believe now that she wanted nothing more to do with him. He would know that he had only to take her into his arms and she was his.

Angrily she pushed herself to her feet. Glancing in his mirror she was shocked by the brightness of her eyes, the heightened colour in her cheeks, but even more deeply by the just-kissed look to her lips. They were deep red and very slightly swollen. A total giveaway.

Moving through to his bathroom she splashed her face with cold water, dabbing it with Saxon's towel. It smelled of his soap—the same scent as his aftershave. The bottle was there on the glass shelf in front of her, his toothbrush too, his razor—and why was she torturing herself by looking at these personal articles?

She dragged a comb—his comb—through her hair and then let herself out, checking carefully that there was no one in the corridor. She hated to think what conclusions would be drawn if they saw her coming out of the surgeon's cabin. She would never be able to hold up her head again.

She took the lift to the Sun Deck, pacing the

boards, drawing in deep breaths of salty evening air, watching the dancing waves, the white wake following the ship, waiting until her pulses slowed before going below to get ready for dinner.

To her relief Mrs Fairfax saw nothing wrong in her appearance, indeed she was more concerned as to why Jancy had been summoned to the hospital. 'The announcement made it sound as though there was something wrong with me! But as I'm fighting fit I knew it was just you the doctor wanted to see.'

Jancy marshalled her thoughts quickly. 'I must admit I was worried, too. I thought you'd been taken ill. As a matter of fact it was nothing much, just a few details he needed for his records.'

'And they wouldn't have waited until he next saw you?' There was a speculative gleam in the woman's eye but to Jancy's relief she did not pursue the subject.

As they dressed for dinner Jancy could not help wondering whether Saxon would be present. She fervently hoped that whatever had called him away would keep him out of the restaurant tonight.

When Giles came to escort them she had to repeat her explanation. He too thought it was odd. 'I don't trust that guy,' he said. 'He fancies you, Jancy. I've seen it in his eyes.'

'Nonsense!' said Jancy, swallowing quickly and hoping he would believe her. 'You're imagining things. He's a doctor and I'm a nurse, that's the reason he shows an interest. There's nothing in it.'

Giles was dressed in a silver-grey lounge suit this evening, with a spotless white shirt and grey tie, but although he looked good he would never match Saxon. Even thinking about the other man made her mouth go dry, but it also made her very angry. She hated Saxon now. She did, *she did*! She must tell herself this over and over again. She must never forget it. He was not worthy of her love.

She took Giles' arm, smiling into his face. 'I'm starving,' she said, 'come on, let's eat.'

But no sooner had she set foot inside the restaurant than she knew her evening was going to be ruined. Saxon was at the table already, his eyes turned in her direction. She pretended not to see him, hanging on to Giles, chattering about the lecture she had attended that afternoon.

Deliberately she smiled into his face, hoping Saxon would take the hint, accept that this was the man she was going to marry—if he asked her! And she was certain he would. He was jealous of Saxon and that was surely a good sign.

The trouble was, she no longer felt that marriage to Giles was the answer. She had once thought a safe secure marriage was all that she wanted, but since meeting Saxon again she knew this was not the case. There would be no rapturous lovemaking with Giles. He would never take her to the heights. It could be a disaster, and would hardly be fair on him.

'I wish you were sitting by me,' grumbled Giles as they neared the table.

'So do I,' said Jancy, squeezing his hand. 'But Saxon sometimes has a quiet word with me about your mother. He likes to keep tabs on her. He's very good in that respect.' This was not strictly true, but she knew Saxon would create a scene if she did move. It could be embarrassing, and would make Giles even more suspicious.

Thankfully Giles said no more, but she sensed he was far from happy, and the fact that Saxon kept his eyes on her face all the time they were walking towards him did not help.

When finally she slipped on to her seat her heart was thudding almost as erratically as it had that afternoon. She wished he did not have this power over her. She could actually feel her fingers trembling as she straightened the folds of her skirt.

Saxon laid a warm firm hand on her arm. 'I'm sorry I had to rush away.'

Jancy felt a tingle at his touch, which grew into a searing like a red hot iron, but her eyes flicked him coldly. 'Don't be sorry, you did me a favour.'

It was ironical, him apologising for such a small thing, when he had hurt her far more deeply all those months ago with no such apology.

She looked at Giles and found his eyes on her, a frown creasing the space between his light sandy brows. He was clearly displeased. She coaxed her lips into a smile, hoping it would reassure him. He responded weakly, but his eyes were angry and it was with reluctance that he turned to answer a question put to him by Debra Forrester.

The couple on Jancy's right were as engrossed in each other as ever and Mrs Fairfax was talking animatedly to Admiral Honeydew. She threw Saxon another savage glance. 'If you were a good host you would start off a conversation that includes everyone, instead of letting us pair off.'

He smiled thinly. 'I'm not complaining.'

'But I am,' she hissed, 'and please take your hand off my arm. Giles is not very pleased about it.'

Saxon obliged but his smile was cynical. 'It will be interesting to hear what he has to say.'

'He ought to kill you,' snapped Jancy.

'I don't think he's man enough for that,' he

returned smoothly. 'If I wanted to take you away from him he'd probably give in without an argument.'

'May the best man win and all that.' Jancy wished she could control her breathing. Her heart felt like a sledge-hammer in her breast. She was not sure whether it was due to the closeness of Saxon or the fact that she was angry—perhaps a mixture of both. 'I think Giles might surprise you. He's tougher than he looks.'

'I would think more of him if he did,' said Saxon. 'I should hate you to marry a man who's unable to defend his future wife.'

'He still doesn't know there was anything between us,' she said, 'and if you behave with the decorum befitting a man in your position he never will.'

She turned to take the menu from the hovering waiter, relieved when Jacob Honeydew said to Saxon, 'Perhaps you can answer this question for me? How many bottles of rum do you reckon are drunk on one of these voyages?'

Jancy was sure he would not know, was surprised when he said, 'I'm not sure about rum alone, but combined with gin and vodka about five hundred bottles on a two-week cruise. Take whisky, though, and there's five hundred drunk of that alone.'

'And how many passengers?' asked the admiral shrewdly.

'Seven hundred and forty, I think,' said Saxon.

Fiona Fairfax looked completely amazed.

'If you're really interested in statistics,' continued the surgeon, 'I believe that about five and a half tons of meat are consumed, six and a half of potatoes, twenty-two thousand bread rolls and two hundred thousand cigarettes are sold, to name but a few. Staggering, isn't it?'

Mrs Fairfax turned to the admiral. 'I can't believe it, I thought you were joking.'

Jancy's brief respite was over. Saxon once again gave his attention to her. 'Have you changed your mind about tomorrow?'

She did not look at him as he spoke, instead she kept her eyes on the menu. 'I think you know the answer to that.' She debated whether to have the smoked rainbow trout or a Miami cocktail, which was described as orange and grapefruit segments in liqueur.

'It's a woman's prerogative,' he urged.

'Is it?' snapped Jancy, deciding on the trout. 'This is one woman who will never change her mind.'

'What can I say to persuade you that you're making a mistake, throwing your life away on Giles Fairfax?'

'Nothing,' she returned tightly. 'I know exactly what I'm doing.' She looked further down the menu. The English turkey was tempting with its chestnut stuffing and cranberry sauce, but so too was the baked smoked gammon ham served with peach slices and a piquant sauce, or the veal escalope cooked and served in foil with sliced ham, gruyere cheese and minced mushrooms.

'You might know what you are doing, but why are you doing it?' he demanded. 'Your response this afternoon told me a lot so don't say that you love Giles because I won't believe you.'

'There are different kinds of love,' she protested. 'I might be attracted to you physically, but that's all. Giles is a kind man and treats me well.'

'And you'd be bored out of your tiny mind

within a few months. What are you doing to yourself, Jancy? Marrying Giles isn't the answer. I'm quite sure his lovemaking doesn't give you complete satisfaction.'

'I don't see that it's any concern of yours.' The gammon won and she gave her order to the patient waiter.

Saxon filled her glass with the wine that he had personally ordered and she took a sip, enjoying the sweet full-bodied flavour.

'To us,' he said softly, raising his glass.

Jancy would have liked more than anything to fling her wine into his face. He was so damned supercilious, so confident that he would win her round. What did he take her for? No man who did the dirty on her would ever be forgiven. 'To us,' she agreed, smiling grimly. 'To a lifetime of living apart.'

'Jancy, Jancy,' he said softly, 'don't torture yourself like this.'

'I'm not torturing myself,' she hissed. 'If anyone's in pain it's you.'

And then the admiral asked Saxon another question and conversation became general. As soon as she had finished her coffee Jancy caught Giles' eye. He too was ready to leave. 'If you'll excuse me,' she said.

At once Saxon stood up and pulled back her chair. Jancy knew it was no accident when his hand brushed the back of her neck. She felt a tingle down her spine but her head was high as she left the restaurant with Giles.

'A breath of fresh air is called for,' he said, looking unlike his usual even-tempered self. Jancy thought she knew what was coming.

They stood at the ship's rail, watching the sun

sink below the horizon, a blood-red ball that set the sea on fire. It was spectacular and dramatic.

'What was that man doing touching you?' he demanded suddenly, spoiling Jancy's pleasure in the scene, his hazel eyes more alive than she could ever remember seeing them. 'Are you sure he's not trying to chat you up?'

'It was nothing like that.' Jancy hoped she sounded convincing. 'He's just sociable, that's all. He knows that you and me are friends.'

'I hope we're more than that,' growled Giles. 'Are you sure you're telling me the truth? He certainly couldn't take his eyes off you. I'm positive that's why he sat you beside him in the first place.'

Jancy swallowed painfully. 'I wouldn't lie to you, Giles, you should know that.'

'I hope not.' He pulled her abruptly against him, kissing her more passionately than he had at any time during their relationship. It was as though he was trying to prove something. Jancy wished she could feel a stronger response. Nothing would matter then, she could settle down happily with Giles. As things were his kisses did nothing and it was difficult to respond.

At length he put her from him, searching her face, a depth of despair behind his eyes. 'You've changed, Jancy,' he stabbed accusingly. 'I knew there was something wrong the other day. I didn't believe your tale about a headache. There's something between you and this guy, isn't there?'

Jancy shook her head wildly. 'No, there isn't, Giles. I can assure you of that. There's nothing between me and the doctor.' Not any longer, she added silently.

'Not yet, maybe,' he growled, 'but you're

attracted to him, aren't you? And he certainly wants you.'

She pressed closer to Giles. 'If he does then it's his bad luck. I have no feelings for him, so don't worry about it.'

'But I do. I love you, you must know that?'

Jancy looked at him sadly and nodded, but could not say the words he was hoping to hear. How could she declare a love that was non-existent? She liked Giles, she liked him a lot. He was a good friend and they had plenty in common. He had helped her over a bad patch. But she did not love him, not how a woman needed to love a man in order to marry him.

'Let's not talk about Saxon Marriot,' she said brightly. 'Let's go and dance. Let's put the whole thing out of our minds.' She swung away from the rail and darted across the deck.

Giles followed slowly but the evening was ruined. Jancy knew that she had not managed to allay his fears.

'I'm really looking forward to tomorrow,' she said, as she sipped her gin and tonic, trying to instil some enthusiasm into her voice. 'Puerto Rico sounds delightful. I've heard it's called Paradise on Earth. Let's hope it lives up to its name.'

Giles did not look so optimistic. The day before he had been eager to discuss their trip, now he appeared totally uninterested. 'It might be better if we joined my mother and the admiral. It's not too late to change our plans.'

But Jancy knew he had been looking forward to exploring on his own and opting out would be tantamount to admitting that there was something wrong. 'I'd rather go with you,' she said, smiling brilliantly.

'In that case,' he shrugged, 'we'll carry on.' But he did not look too happy and when Jancy went to bed he stayed on deck. She guessed he needed to think things over and hoped she had convinced him there was nothing between her and Saxon. The remainder of the cruise would be hellishly uncomfortable if he was still suspicious.

It was a long time before Jancy slept but once she did manage it she did not wake until early morning. The ship had dropped her anchors during the night and she missed the constant hum of the engines. All seemed strangely silent and still, as though something dramatic was going to happen! It was a figment of her imagination, she knew, yet she could not help feeling uneasy.

On this occasion Jancy ate her breakfast in the cabin with her employer and did not think it strange when Giles failed to put in an appearance. He would be taking his early morning jog before they disembarked. Nothing would stop him doing that.

When the announcement was made for all those joining the excursion to assemble in the Bureau Lobby the admiral collected Mrs Fairfax and they left.

Shortly afterwards a sharp rap on the door heralded Giles' arrival. But it was a different Giles who stood there, his face grim, his whole body tense. He had certainly not been jogging.

'I want a word with you,' he said at once, pushing her backwards into the cabin and closing the door firmly.

Jancy's heart fell. It could only be about Saxon. There was absolutely no other reason why Giles should be angry with her.

'You lied to me,' he accused harshly, 'when you

said there was nothing between you and the surgeon.'

Jancy's beautiful green eyes widened. 'Giles, there's nothing between us, I can assure you of that.'

'Then why does he tell me differently?' His face was a deep angry red, his whole stance that of a man in the grip of an emotion that was swiftly getting the better of him.

Jancy blinked. 'You've been talking to Saxon?'

'I went to see him first thing this morning. I couldn't sleep last night for thinking about it. I believed you, fool that I was, but I knew Saxon Marriot had more than a smattering of interest. I wanted to put him right, let him know that you were my girl and not available.'

Jancy licked her suddenly dry lips, swallowing painfully. 'And what did he say?' Her voice was low and husky, almost a whisper.

'That you had once been lovers,' he snarled.

Jancy gasped.

'Why did you let me believe that you'd never met before?'

'I didn't say that.' Jancy touched his arm tentatively but he snatched away as though he could no longer bear her near him.

'But you implied it. Why didn't you tell me you'd had an affair?'

'Because I hadn't,' protested Jancy angrily. 'We were friends, I'll admit that. We were—close. But we were never lovers.'

He looked at her coldly. 'Do you expect me to accept that after you lied about knowing him?'

'I didn't lie,' cried Jancy, her voice full of pain.

'Evading the issue amounts to the same thing.'

'I saw no point in telling you,' she continued

softly. 'It's all been over so long.' Why was her integrity always questioned? First Saxon, now Giles. Couldn't either of them accept her for what she was?

Giles rubbed his chin ruefully. 'Saxon Marriot certainly has a more positive way of making me believe things.'

'You mean he hit you?' She looked at him more closely, frowning when she saw the redness.

Giles grimaced. 'He took me by surprise, otherwise I'd have flattened him.'

'But why? How did it come to that?' Jancy pictured the two men grappling in Saxon's cabin. Over her! It was flattering, but distressing all the same.

'He tried to tell me that you were still his girl. That he had no intention of letting you go. I told him it was rubbish, that even if you'd once been his lover he no longer had any hold over you. I said you loved me—and that we were going to get married?' He looked at her anxiously, questioningly.

'I told him much the same myself,' admitted Jancy. 'I don't suppose he believed you any more than he did me?'

Giles shook his head savagely. 'He said you didn't know what was good for you. I don't know who the hell he thinks he is. He said that no one like me would ever have you. That you loved him even though you won't admit it, and that he won't rest until you go back to him.'

Jancy's eyes were saucer-like. 'Of all the nerve! I have a mind of my own, Giles. I shall never go back to Saxon Marriot. He said some pretty hurtful things to me. I shall never forgive him, ever.'

Giles looked at her sadly, his anger slowly

dissipating. 'I wish I could believe you.'

'You can, I assure you.'

He shook his head, again rubbing his injured chin. 'Saxon Marriot was convincing when he said you were his woman. He must know you better than I do if he's so sure you'll go back to him.'

Jancy shrugged, trying to look unconcerned. 'Maybe that's what he thinks, but it's not what's going to happen. He gave up all rights to me. I'd forgotten about him,' she lied, 'until he turned up here. I wish he hadn't.'

'Me, too,' said Giles faintly, 'but even if what you say is true it won't alter the way *he* feels. He'll ruin the whole cruise.'

'We won't let him,' said Jancy, winding her arms around Giles' waist. 'I have no intention of giving him another chance. Let's forget him. Let's not spoil this day. Puerto Rico is waiting for us, I can't wait to explore.'

He heaved a sigh. 'You still want to come with me?'

'Of course I do,' she assured him.

'It won't be easy to forget some of the things he said. He's one hell of a determined man, Jancy.'

She shook her head. 'You're as strong as he, and I'm on your side. Two against one. We've got to win.' She pressed a kiss to his cheek and he groaned and crushed her to him.

Jancy knew she was making a big mistake, encouraging Giles, but what else could she do? There was no way she would go back to Saxon. He had disillusioned her completely. He was best out of her life altogether.

Puerto Rico was indeed a beautiful island. They spent the first hour exploring the old part of the city near the harbour. It was almost completely surrounded by sea and still partially encircled with stone walls.

To begin with the atmosphere between them was tense, but gradually Giles relaxed. He was still a little distant, but it was not sufficient to spoil the day.

Jancy was fascinated by the overhanging balconies with their wrought iron railings, roads paved with blue tiles which, she discovered, had been brought to the island as ballast on the ships of *conquistadores*.

They came across unexpected courtyards and dark narrow alleys leading to the sea. The roads were crowded. There were small chapels and large churches and they paid a brief visit to the great fortress of El Morro built in the middle of the sixteenth century.

Jancy also managed to persuade Giles that a visit to the cathedral of St John was a must, even though he was anxious to explore the rest of the island.

In the Plaza Colon was a giant statue of Columbus who had discovered the island in the fifteenth century. There were art galleries and craft centres and Jancy exclaimed over the tortoiseshell jewellery, the distinctive vivid pottery, but it was the exquisite island embroidery she fell in love with, unable to resist purchasing a blouse as a memento of her visit.

She was also attracted, as were several dozen other people, by a man peeling oranges in the street. He had a cart piled high with the fruit and in an amazingly short space of time cut a long continuous strip of peel from each one, before making a hole in the top for his customers to drink the juice. Jancy simply had to have one.

But Giles was impatient to move on. The

traffic jams were like Regent Street in the rush hour, cars speeding in every direction, seeming to think they were the only ones on the road. Jancy was convinced they would have an accident, but somehow they made it, and *out on the island*, as the Puerto Ricans termed it, was like being in a different world. There were smooth well-made roads criss-crossing it, each bearing a number, so that armed with a map there was no chance of them getting lost.

There seemed to be a church on every hill top and they passed houses surrounded by trees, which were apparently the homes of the *jibaros*, Puerto Rican peasants. There were road menders wearing blue blouses and red scarves tied under wide straw hats.

Jancy was thrilled with the wonderful colours all about them. Pink bougainvillaea and red hibiscus, yellow flowering vines; but most vivid of all were the flowering trees. The pink and yellow poiu, the dazzling white of the frangipani, the glowing scarlet cups of the African tulips, and the yellow-orange of oleander.

Most predominant of all was the flamboyant tree—the island's national flower, called lovingly, Red Velvet. Its flaunting scarlet blossoms swathed the hillsides. It was the most spectacular sight Jancy had ever seen.

'Are we going to the rain forest?' she asked, knowing it was on the ship's itinerary, and a very popular tourist area. She felt Giles might want to avoid it.

'You bet,' he said strongly. 'El Yunque is the second highest peak in the Cordillera Central Mountain Range, did you know? I hope you've put your walking shoes on?'

Jancy laughed. He sounded more like his old self. 'You're forgetting I attended the port talk. There's a road up the mountain, you can't fool me.' She had not heard all that was said, due to the disturbing influence of Saxon, but that much she knew.

She wondered where Saxon was now. Whether he had stayed on the *Ocean Queen* or gone somewhere on his own. She was glad Giles had tackled him, because it proved he was a man and not the mouse Saxon had hinted at.

As they began their ascent it was like being in a different world. Waterfalls cascaded prettily, tree trunks were festooned with climbing vines. There were tree ferns thirty feet high, and wild parrots gave a brilliant flash of colour as they flew through the branches. It was a cool and tranquil place despite the steady stream of cars.

'Did you know,' asked Giles, 'that the rainfall here is approximately a hundred and eighty three inches a year? It's remarkable when you consider San Juan has less than a third of that amount, and in the extreme south it's semi-desert. What an island of contrasts.'

'Who told you?' asked Jancy, trying to recall whether they had mentioned this at the lecture.

'I've done my homework,' he smiled. 'It's no good coming to a place like this and knowing nothing about it. As Samuel Johnson once said, "A man must carry knowledge with him if he would bring home knowledge." See those trees.' He pointed suddenly. 'They are asubo, or bulletwood, and are almost extinct. Many of the old houses in San Juan were built from this wood because it's resistant to both the climate and insects. It's apparently so valuable that when old houses are pulled down the wood is carefully stored by the Institute of Puerto Rican Culture to re-use on preservation projects.'

Jancy was impressed. Giles was telling her as much, she was sure, as Saxon would have done, and he seemed to have quite got over his earlier anger.

From the observation tower at the summit of El Yunque the view was superb. The green forest fell away beneath them and the mountain range strode into the distance like the ridged back of a giant dragon. Giles casually rested his arm about Jancy's shoulders. 'Quite something, isn't it?'

She nodded, the sheer incredible beauty robbing her of speech. Faintly came the damning thought that she would like to share it with Saxon. 'Let's eat,' she said hurriedly, cursing him for intruding into this moment.

The summit restaurant served excellent food and they could still enjoy the panorama from the terrace. Jancy had her first taste of *tostones*. Giles, continually amazing her by his knowledge, said, 'They're made from plantains, the same genus as the banana. The fruit is washed, boiled, pounded into inch-long pieces and then fried in olive oil.'

'They taste like banana-flavoured potato crisps,' laughed Jancy. 'They're different, but I'm not sure I like them. The chicken's delicious, though.' And when for dessert she tried crystallised guavas served with goat's cheese to counteract the excessive sweetness, she exclaimed, 'These are truly fantastic, Giles, you really ought to try some.'

He shook his head, laughing. 'Too sweet for me, but if you want to get fat, carry on.'

Jancy pulled a face. 'I've no doubt you'll be running round the decks tomorrow morning to get rid of all the excess calories you've eaten. You'll never put on weight, that's for sure.' She was glad he was back to his old self.

On their way down the mountain Jancy spotted wild orchids and other exotic flowers she had missed on the way up. There was so much to see and exclaim over.

The cataracts seemed to fall even more steeply—and suddenly it rained! It lasted for no more than ten minutes but was steady and heavy. Giles stopped the car and they listened to it drumming on the roof, water streaming down the windows, distorting their vision.

When the sun came out again it transformed the rain forest with its scintillating shafts of light. It was a magical wonderland and appeared to weave its spell over Giles as much as it did Jancy.

'I never expected our day to turn out like this.' He half turned towards her. 'After this morning I thought it was all over. I wish you'd told me about him, Jancy. I feel very hurt.'

'I'm sorry,' she whispered. 'It was a shock to me when I discovered he was the ship's surgeon. I'd been doing my best to forget him.'

'And you're sure you are over him now? He left me in no doubt that he intended taking you away from me and marrying you.'

Jancy's heart jerked painfully. It had never occurred to her that Saxon was so serious. At one time marriage was all that she had wanted, but now it was a risk she could never take.

He was a man of violent moods, who acted first and thought later. If they married and there was another misunderstanding he would react equally as violently—and it would be too late then for her to do anything about it. He would be sheer hell to live with under those circumstances.

'He said that?' she queried, open-mouthed.

'He was very positive,' said Giles, flexing his jaw on which the faint shadow of a bruise was beginning to show.

'It takes two to make a marriage,' declared Jancy strongly, 'and no way am I going to marry that man.'

Giles heaved a sigh and gathered her to him. 'Jancy, darling, you don't know how glad I am to hear you say that. I had no intention just yet of asking you to marry me, but I fear Saxon has forced my hand. Will you marry me? Say yes, and I'll make sure you never want for anything.'

Jancy looked into his face; there was pain and anxiety in his eyes, a tension that she had never known before. He was such an easy-going person, always enjoying life to the full, that it disturbed her to see him upset like this.

But was marriage to Giles the answer? Subconsciously she would always compare him to Saxon. The marriage would be tolerably happy, she had no doubt about that, and if it failed it would be entirely her fault.

She would have liked more time to think about it. If she said no now he would immediately jump to the conclusion that she still had some feelings for Saxon. On the other hand, if she said yes, she would be commmitted, and she was fond enough of Giles not to want to hurt him by backing out.

Contrarily getting herself engaged to Giles would confirm what they had both told Saxon. It could be the answer—and really, would marrying Giles be such a bad thing? Had Saxon not re-entered her life she would have seriously considered it.

'I'm waiting, Jancy?'

She gave a wry smile and nodded. 'Yes, Giles, I will marry you.'

He groaned and gave her a bear-like hug, but his relief made her feel guilty. Her heart felt as heavy as lead, her whole body weighed down with a burden too monumental to carry. She ought to retract—now—before it went any further. This was not the solution.

'You won't regret this, Jancy, I promise—and Mother will be so pleased too.'

His mother? She wasn't marrying his mother, for heaven's sake! Her employer had never made any secret of the fact that she thought they were good for each other. The woman would be overjoyed. But it also meant that if she, Jancy, did not go through with it, she would not only have Giles' distress to cope with, she would lose her job too. Mrs Fairfax would never forgive her for hurting her son.

Determinedly, however, she pushed these thoughts to the back of her mind and concentrated on returning Giles' kisses with as much ardour as she could muster. It was nothing like the response she gave Saxon, there were no angels singing in her head, but he seemed satisfied, sitting back in his seat a few minutes later, smiling blissfully.

'I could fight Goliath now,' he said. 'You've made me the happiest man alive.' He started the car and they continued their descent of El Yunque.

'I wonder if your mother's enjoying herself,' said Jancy. 'I thought we might have seen them. I hope the admiral's looking after her. Do you think anything will come of their relationship? How do you fancy him as your stepfather?'

Giles shrugged. 'So long as mother's happy it

doesn't really matter, although I think you're being a bit premature. These holiday things rarely last.'

'I think he's nice,' said Jancy, 'and good for her.' She glanced at her watch. They still had a couple of hours before they need return. 'What shall we do now? I wish I'd packed my bikini. We could have found a quiet beach and gone swimming.'

'Tomorrow in Antigua we'll do that,' promised Giles, glancing at her affectionately. 'I thought we'd go horse riding. They have these marvellous Paso Finos. They're very small thoroughbreds developed from the Andalusians. I believe they're an education to ride because they have an exceptionally smooth gait.'

Jancy had done no riding since her early teens but nodded enthusiastically. 'I remember seeing them on television once, at some horse show in New York. A horsey friend of mine made a point of telling me about them.'

'That's right,' said Giles. 'Apparently the test of a good Paso Fino rider is that he can carry a full glass of water without spilling a drop, and the reason they have such a smooth walk is that the hind foot strikes the ground fractionally before the front.'

Jancy was excited at the prospect of riding these beautiful horses—and was not disappointed. They spent the next hour cantering along the deeply shaded tracks by the sea. Giles was tremendously happy, singing in his deep baritone voice. Jancy found his pleasure infectious and was sorry when it was time to go back to the ship. She was not looking forward to her next meeting with Saxon.

After showering Jancy went topside to anxiously await her employer's return, hoping Mrs Fairfax had not overdone it. After all, she was supposed to be looking after her, it was what she was being paid for.

When the coach came into view she felt a sense of relief, but before it dropped off its passengers a *público* screamed to a halt in front of it. A *público*, Jancy had discovered, was a sort of taxi, except that it ran on more or less scheduled runs and was a cheap way of seeing the island.

Jancy watched with interest to see who had toured Puerto Rico by this manner, taken aback when she saw Saxon unfold himself from the vehicle. She found it difficult to believe that he had gone alone on one of these trips, and was not surprised when he turned back into the car and helped out his companion.

It was none other then Debra Forrester! Obviously the fact that she was married made no difference. Jancy wondered whether he had deliberately asked her out because of his fracas with Giles, needing female company to soothe him. Considering he had made a point of telling Giles that she, Jancy, was his woman it did not make much sense.

A stab of jealousy pierced her. Debra had hidden none of her feelings for the doctor and Jancy could well imagine the kind of day she had had. The woman must have thought her luck was in. Even as she watched Saxon draped an arm casually about Debra Forrester's shoulders, leading her back to the ship, his dark head bent low to catch what she was saying.

Jancy knew she ought not to be jealous when she did not want Saxon for herself, that she should not resent him taking out another woman. But she did, and the fact that she had committed herself to a loveless marriage made it harder to bear.

She swung away from the rail and almost ran to her cabin, desperate to avoid Saxon. She sat on the edge of the bed-settee, her fingers clenched into balls at her side. She felt cold and could not stop herself from wondering whether he had kissed Debra, whether Debra had invited him back to her cabin. In her own mind Jancy was certain that this banker's wife would not reject him.

At dinner tonight she would watch them closely. If anything had happened between them she would see it on the woman's face. There would be that eye contact for one thing, and Debra would glow, looking like a new woman. Jancy knew it all.

Her lips were angrily compressed when the door suddenly opened. Mrs Fairfax skipped into the room—or that was what it seemed like to Jancy.

Forcing a smile she marvelled at the change in her employer. The woman looked like a young girl again. There was a sparkle to her eyes, animation to her face. Jancy did not have to ask whether she had had a good day.

'You look wonderful,' she said, 'and here was I worrying whether I ought to have let you go off alone.'

'I've had a marvellous time,' said Fiona Fairfax, easing off her shoes and lowering herself on to the settee beside Jancy. 'Jacob's such a darling man.' She looked at her nurse shrewdly. 'But you don't look as though you've had such a good day. Have you and Giles quarrelled?'

Now was certainly not the time to tell her they had just got engaged. Such an announcement should be accompanied by a smile as brilliant as her employer's had been when she entered the cabin. But she made an effort to brighten up. 'Not at all, I've thoroughly enjoyed myself. We went to the Rain Forest after exploring San Juan, and then went horse riding. It's been super.'

Mrs Fairfax gave Jancy a long considering look but, as usual, kept her thoughts to herself. 'I could do iwth a cup of tea. Organise it for me, there's a love.'

Jancy was glad of something to do, and hoped that she would be able to have a word with Giles before he broke the news. It had been a mistake letting Mrs Fairfax catch her with that angry expression on her face.

All too soon it was time to get ready for dinner. Jancy dressed with care. It was wonderful having so many new dresses to choose from. She selected a shimmering green that was the colour of her eyes, sweeping up her thick copper hair into a neat chignon, allowing tendrils to escape in her nape, defiantly adding a silk rose in matching green.

Giles gave her an appraising look when he came in to collect the two women. 'You look good enough to eat,' he said, 'and you too, Mother. I've certainly no need to ask how your day's gone.'

Mrs Fairfax gave a self-satisfied smile. 'Jacob's quite something. I feel years younger.'

'Good for you,' he said warmly. 'I like Jacob, too. I'm so glad you've met someone nearer your own age.'

His mother pulled a face. 'So that you won't have to spend so much of your time with me? Don't think I can't see through you, my boy. How did your day go? Jancy was——'

Afraid of what she might be going to say Jancy interrupted quickly. 'I think we ought to go. The admiral will be waiting.'

'But I haven't told Mother our good news yet, Jancy.'

Mrs Fairfax had gone back into her bedroom to collect her handbag and missed Giles' remark. Jancy said quietly, 'I think we ought to wait.'

He frowned momentarily, then his brow cleared. 'You're right, it's far too important an announcement to be rushed. You're also right about the admiral. I've never seen her like this before. Maybe I ought to check him out, make sure he's good enough for her.'

'I reckon he's the most impeccable man she's likely to meet,' said Jancy. 'And won't she have something to tell her friends, a retired admiral, no less. I think it's terrific.'

'Maybe we'll have a double wedding,' grinned Giles, squeezing her hand.

'Come along, Giles, what are we waiting for?' Mrs Fairfax bustled out of the cabin and they trailed behind. Giles shook his head and laughed. 'Isn't she the limit?'

As they walked he said, 'I'm going to insist that you sit by me in future. Debra won't object, and Saxon can do nothing about it if we present a united front.'

'As a matter of fact he's been out with Debra today,' informed Jancy. 'I saw them coming back when I was looking for your mother.'

'And you didn't mind?' Giles' eyes narrowed. 'You are sure you're over him? I don't want to make another fool of myself.'

Jancy swallowed hard. 'I'm sure.' She hated herself for lying, but seeing Saxon with Debra had driven a knife into her heart. She would never get over Saxon Marriot, not as long as she lived.

As always when they entered the restaurant Jancy looked straight towards their table, unaware that she gripped Giles' hand more tightly than usual. When at first she could not see Saxon's dark handsome face standing out from every one else she thought he was merely hidden from sight. It was not until they actually reached the table that she discovered his seat was empty.

Relief flooded over her. She had keyed herself up for this meeting and now it looked as though Saxon's work had done her a good turn. It could only be duty that kept him away.

Debra Forrester too was missing so Giles settled Jancy beside him, and when the banker's wife eventually turned up she took Jancy's old seat without demur. The woman looked particularly radiant and Jancy knew that she had guessed correctly.

For once Jancy thoroughly enjoyed the meal, listening to Admiral Honeydew's account of a trip he had made to the Caribbean many years earlier. Even the American company president joined in the conversation. She discovered he had quite a wit and kept them laughing at the things he said.

During the night the ship steamed its way towards Antigua. Jancy was unable to sleep, however. She kept thinking about Saxon's declaration that he was going to marry her. An ambiguous statement if ever there was one. She would never marry him. Never! Even though she loved him it was a risk she dare not take. Besides, he had proved how little he cared by taking out Debra Forrester.

The next morning, feeling drained of all energy, Jancy showered and dressed before popping her head round the door of her employer's cabin.

Mrs Fairfax's eyes were closed, her face pale, a faint tinge of blue round her bloodless lips. Jancy's heart lurched and she moved quickly into the room.

CHAPTER FIVE

MRS Fairfax opened her eyes as Jancy approached, giving her a weak apologetic smile. 'I think I did too much yesterday.'

'I'll send for the doctor.' Jancy did not like the look of her at all.

'And perhaps you'll let Jacob know? He'll be so disappointed. He was really looking forward to today.'

When Jancy rang the hospital Saxon himself answered. 'Mrs Fairfax is not feeling well,' she said. 'I'd like you to take a look at her.'

'I'll be there at once.' His voice was brisk and the phone went dead. Jancy was alarmed to discover that that brief moment of speaking to him had been enough to quicken her pulse rate. She wondered achingly whether she would ever get over him.

Within a minute Saxon was at the door. Jancy let him in, taking him straight through to Mrs Fairfax. He was at his most professional. After a thorough examination he announced he was not happy with her. 'You must take things easy. None of this island hopping for you, I'm afraid.'

Mrs Fairfax looked disappointed. 'But——'

'But nothing,' he cut in. 'There's still plenty happening on board. We normally have entertainers from each island we visit, and of course there's the usual cards and indoor games—and a film. You can have just as good a time here without any unnecessary exertion.'

The woman sighed, but nodded. 'You're right, of course, doctor.'

When he turned to go he beckoned Jancy to follow him into the outer cabin, closing the connecting door. 'I'd like you to come along and collect some tablets for your employer. She needs calming down, she's more excited than is good for her.'

'It's the admiral,' said Jancy.

He nodded. 'With her heart condition she needs to take care. I'm not saying she should remain idle, moderate exercise is good for her, but she's in no state to go galloping around with Jacob Honeydew. He's a fit man for his age.'

'I think he should be told about her heart,' said Jancy. 'I doubt Mrs Fairfax has said anything. She'd probably think it would ruin her chances.'

'I'll do it,' he said, and then his professional manner disappeared. 'And how about you? How did your day go yesterday?'

Jancy jutted her chin. 'I had a marvellous time. Puerto Rico is beautiful. We went to the Rain Forest and had lunch at the restaurant at the top, and then went horse riding. Aren't those Paso Finos lovely?'

'Quit stalling, Jancy,' he said tightly. 'You know very well what I mean.'

'If you're wondering whether Giles told me about your showdown, he did. And I think you have a nerve telling him you intend marrying me. Surely I should be the one to make the choice? I'm going to marry Giles, Saxon, and there is nothing you can do about it.'

He looked at her savagely and the power in the blue eyes turned Jancy's limbs to water. He was the one man in the world who had brought her alive, who had taught her the meaning of the word love. Yet he had thought it was all an act, that she had deliberately set out to ensnare him. He had cast her out of his life with no thought at all for her own feelings.

'Perhaps Giles didn't get the message?' he snarled. 'Or perhaps he failed to realise how determined I can be once my mind is made up?'

'Oh, he did,' said Jancy. 'When a man almost has his jaw broken he gets the message all right. You were very brutal. I'm sure it wasn't necessary.'

'Giles was aggressive,' returned Saxon bitterly. 'Don't expect me to apologise because I'll do it again if necessary.'

Jancy threw him an angry look. 'He certainly wouldn't take it lying down that you were after his girl. I'd only just convinced him that I wanted nothing to do with you.'

'But you hadn't confessed that we'd had an earlier relationship. You should have seen his face.' He looked grimly pleased.

'I've no doubt you took the greatest delight in rubbing it in?'

'I spoke the truth,' he said. 'I'm not going to let you marry Giles.'

Her eyes flashed. 'I'm certainly not going to marry you.'

'Oh, yes you are. I don't care how long it takes me to persuade you, but in the end I shall win.'

Jancy swung away. 'Don't you think we ought to go and get those tablets?'

He put a restraining hand on her arm. 'Are you afraid of me, Jancy?'

She looked at him sharply. Afraid of herself, yes; afraid of her feelings. But afraid of Saxon? It surprised her to discover she was not sure. Perhaps she was afraid of what he could do to her—of the power he wielded over her. 'Why should I be afraid of you?' she challenged. 'We both have jobs to do, I suggest we get on with them.' Her voice told him that she meant what she said, that there were to be no repeats of the scene which had almost finished with him making love to her.

He said no more and she quickly moved to the door. In the hospital he gave instructions to one of his nurses who counted out the prescribed number of tablets. Jancy stood rigidly just inside the room. At least here they could not converse on a personal level. He sat at his desk and filled in a report. The nurse handed Jancy the tablets and he did not even look up as she left.

When she got back to their cabin Giles was with his mother. 'For goodness' sake, Jancy,' exclaimed Mrs Fairfax, 'tell Giles there's nothing wrong with me that a short rest won't cure. I believe he thinks I'm dying.'

Jancy smiled at Giles. 'Your mother needs to slow down, that's all. She overdid it yesterday.'

Giles did not look convinced, although he nodded slowly.

'Have you told Jacob yet, Jancy?' asked Mrs Fairfax, dismissing her son. 'He's probably getting ready right now for our trip around Antigua.'

'Saxon—er, the doctor, said he'd do it.'

Mrs Fairfax's eyes shot wide. 'He'll tell him what's wrong.'

'I think he should know,' said Jancy. 'It's no good him dragging you off every time we stop if you're not up to it.'

'Yes, but——'

Giles cut in. 'If he thinks as much of you as he

seems to do it will make no difference. You're a fool not to have told him.'

'No woman likes to feel she's past it,' grumbled his mother. 'I don't want to be a drag on Jacob. He really likes getting out and renewing his acquaintance with places he's seen before.'

'What you have to ask yourself,' said Giles kindly, 'is whether your own health comes before pleasing the admiral. You can't have the best of both worlds.'

'You're right, of course,' replied his mother despondently, settling down between the sheets and turning her face to the wall.

Giles looked at Jancy helplessly and they left the room. Over breakfast he said, 'I don't really like leaving my mother in the condition she's in, but I would like to see Nelson's Dockyard.'

'There's no reason why you shouldn't go.' Jancy bit into a flaky croissant. 'There's nothing you can do. I shall stay here, naturally, it's my duty. I should have gone with her yesterday, made sure she didn't do too much.'

Giles nodded. 'I feel guilty, too. I was thinking only of myself when I dragged you away. Are you sure you won't mind if I go alone?'

Jancy smiled at his concern. 'Of course not. Enjoy yourself. This is your holiday.'

'Yours too.'

'Not really,' she said. 'I'm here to work. I'm your mother's nurse. I think you forget that.'

'I do,' he admitted wryly. 'You're just Jancy to me. My special girl. My fiancée now.'

'I'm glad we didn't tell your mother,' said Jancy, 'or I'd have felt it was the excitement over us that made her ill. I think we ought to keep it to ourselves for a bit longer.'

He did not look too happy but nodded his agreement, and when Jancy returned to the cabin the admiral was anxiously pacing up and down looking as worried as Giles had earlier. 'Why the devil didn't you tell me?' he boomed, the moment Jancy set foot inside. 'I never realised you were Fiona's nurse. I thought you were her future daughter-in-law.'

Jancy grimaced. She was unaware that her employer had actually put her hopes and dreams into words. 'I'm Mrs Fairfax's nurse first and foremost. I'm afraid I neglected my duty yesterday. I certainly shan't do it again.'

'It was my own fault,' interrupted Mrs Fairfax, and to Jacob, 'I should have told you that I'm not as strong as I look.'

'You certainly should,' he said firmly, and then on a quieter note, 'Now I do know it will be my pleasure, dear lady, to look after you.' He waved his hand imperiously in Jancy's direction. 'You are dismissed. Go and enjoy yourself with that young man of yours.'

Jancy smiled and left the room. Mrs Fairfax already looked one hundred per cent better, but she had no intention of going off for the day and leaving her again. She would pop in now and then to make sure the woman was behaving herself.

On the Sun Deck she lay down, appreciating the unaccustomed luxury of having it to herself. The Caribbean sun soaked into her skin. She was developing a healthy tan and although this cruise was primarily for Mrs Fairfax's benefit she was getting something out of it too. If it wasn't for Saxon her happiness would be complete.

She wondered whether he had gone ashore. It seemed that most people had. There were very few left on board. She closed her eyes and drifted into a light sleep, waking only when she felt someone touch her arm.

When she looked up Saxon was perched on the edge of the lounger next to her, still in the black trousers and white shirt that were his uniform. Jancy sat up at once. 'Is Mrs Fairfax worse?'

He smiled, shaking his head. 'She's fine. The admiral is keeping her company. There's nothing to worry about in that direction.'

'Then why are you here?'

'Isn't that obvious? We're two lonely souls. I thought we could keep each other company. I thought I might persuade you to go ashore with me?'

Jancy stared at him coldly, ignoring the clamour of her pulses, regretful it was never like this with Giles. Marriage to him could be a disaster. There would be no excitement, and after the newness had worn off, what then? Life could be totally boring. 'You must know what my answer will be.'

'Unfortunately, yes, so I took the liberty of asking Mrs Fairfax. She was somewhat surprised that you were still here. She thought you'd gone ashore with her son.'

'You did what?' Jancy jerked to a sitting position, eyeing him indignantly. 'You had no right. What did she say? And what do you think Giles will do if I go with you?'

'He knows very well what my intentions are,' he returned smoothly, 'but I told his mother I need to pick up some urgent medical supplies. As I must leave someone on duty here and two signatures are required before I can get hold of the stuff, I need you as a qualified nurse to accompany me.'

'And she fell for that?' Jancy was incredulous. 'She must be mad.'

'I somehow think,' said Saxon, 'that she was relieved you'd be out of her hair. She wants to be alone with her admiral, without fear of you poking your nose in every few minutes. She certainly didn't need much persuading.'

'Well, I'm sorry,' said Jancy tightly, 'but you've wasted your efforts. You'll never convince me that going anywhere with you is the right thing. I intend remaining here and there is nothing you can do about it.'

She jumped to her feet, her face ablaze with anger. 'Go ashore yourself, Mr Marriot, and pick up your phoney medical supplies.' With that she spun on her heel and fled down the steps, not caring where she went so long as she got away.

If he was going to badger her like this for the rest of the voyage it would be intolerable. She wished now she had gone with Giles, that she hadn't let her conscience dictate. The admiral was perfectly capable of looking after Mrs Fairfax.

In the Flamingo Bar she ordered herself a vodka and tonic, half expecting Saxon to follow, relieved when he didn't. She sipped her drink, glancing around the empty room. It was amazing how different it looked without the passengers.

Its coral pink and white decor was easy on the eye but it was the passengers that brought it to life, created the atmosphere that was the very essence of a cruise. Most of the time it was like one big party, or at least it had been before she discovered Saxon's presence. Now it was like the morning after.

Her drink finished she wandered below to the gymnasium, spending her anger on the exercise bicycle, pedalling furiously, trying to cast all thoughts of Saxon Marriot from her mind. She sweated in the sauna, took a swim in the heated pool, and eventually decided to go and see how Mrs Fairfax was feeling.

Unfortunately her path took her past the hospital and she cursed when the door opened and Saxon came out. He looked surprised to see her but when she tried to ignore him he caught her arm in a vice-like grip.

'Don't say you were going past without calling in to see me?' His voice dripped sarcasm.

'What happened to those urgent medical supplies you so desperately needed?' she asked. 'Why aren't you ashore fetching them?'

His eyes narrowed. 'You know as well as I do that it was an excuse.'

She tried in vain to pull herself free. 'You're hurting my arm.'

His grip merely tightened. 'You can't escape me, Jancy. Your response the other day told me exactly how you feel. Even though your tongue lies your heart speaks the truth.'

'As I said then,' snapped Jancy, 'it's nothing more than physical. What are you after, an affair?'

'I'm trying to persuade you,' he said with exaggerated patience, 'that I'm the one you love, not that half a man who likes to pretend he's tough.'

'Let's leave Giles out of this,' retorted Jancy. 'I did love you once, but it's gone now. You effectively destroyed all my feelings.'

'Liar!' he bit out savagely. 'And marrying Giles is certainly not the solution.'

'It's my life,' cried Jancy bitterly, still trying to pull free. 'Let me go, Saxon, this minute. You can't do this to me, I won't let you.'

He smiled wickedly. 'When I'm good and ready.

It's unlikely we'll be disturbed. Perhaps it was providence that sent you.' He dragged her protestingly to his cabin, closing the door firmly behind them.

Jancy could not help but remember the last time and felt panic rise in her throat. Once Saxon began attacking her defences there was little chance she would be able to hide the true state of her feelings.

But she let none of her fears show, turning to face him, her hands clasped behind her back so that he should not see their nervous twisting. 'What do you propose doing now you've got me here?' she asked defiantly, her chin jutting, her green eyes flashing hostilely.

'Persuade you that marrying me is the best thing you can do.' He stood a couple of yards away from her, still the most sensually attractive male she had ever met. He took off his tie and unbuttoned his shirt, revealing the golden brown of his hard chest, the fine scattering of dark hairs through which she had run her fingers countless times.

Jancy felt drugged simply looking at him. 'Forcing me will not help.'

'We have so little time together,' he said. 'Now is an ideal opportunity to convince you that I'm the right man.'

'You'll never do that,' she cried. 'You wouldn't hesitate to kick me out of your life again if we had another misunderstanding. It's not a chance I'm going to give you.'

'I want you,' he said softly, urgently.

'Then that's your hard luck,' she snapped, her eyes wildly furious, 'because I no longer have any feelings for you. When are you going to take notice of what I say and stop pestering me? You're wasting not only your own time but mine.' She shook her head angrily, copper hair flying. 'It's over, Saxon. Over, over, *over*.'

'No,' he flung loudly, 'I refuse to believe you. You're still hurt, that's all.' He moved swiftly and pulled her into his arms. 'Let me prove that I'm a better man than Giles. I want you, Jancy. I want you so badly it's destroying me. Doesn't that tell you anything?'

She pulled back as far as the restricting circle of his arms would allow. 'No, Saxon, I'm afraid it doesn't. It tells me precisely nothing.'

'You bitch!' he grated harshly. 'Why don't you stop fighting? Why don't you relax and let me give you what we both know you want?'

Jancy was achingly aware of the vibrant power of his body. She knew that if he did not let her go all would be lost. Already her adrenalin was pumping, desire spiralling through her, feelings she tried so hard to suppress flooding to the surface. It was incredible after the way he had treated her that he still had the power to set her on fire.

'What *you* want,' she thrust, 'not me! I have no intention of ending up in your bed.'

He looked pained. 'I'd settle for your company. I've missed you like hell.'

Jancy glanced at him scathingly. 'It was your choice.'

'I've admitted I was in the wrong,' he said. 'What else do you expect me to say?'

'I expect you to leave me alone.'

'I can't, Jancy. I can't stand by and watch you ruin your life. I want you to marry me.' His arms tightened and his mouth swooped on hers.

Jancy turned her head. 'Go to hell,' she said thickly.

He tensed, and then suddenly, surprisingly, let her go. His face was hard as he walked over to his drinks cupboard and poured himself a generous measure of whisky which he downed in one swallow. 'Marry Giles and you'll be as frustrated as hell in no time at all.'

'You're being extremely insulting,' she said cuttingly. 'Nothing gives you the right to speak to me like that.'

'Not even what we once had going for us?'

She shook her head. 'Not even that.'

'I don't like to see you throw your life away.' He poured himself another drink and she noticed that his hands were not quite steady, a nervous tic appearing in his jaw.

'You care nothing about me,' she flung incautiously. 'All you care about is your own precious male ego. You didn't like it when you thought I'd made a fool of you, that's the top and bottom of it. It's a pity I ever went to my sister's engagement party. I'd have been a whole lot better off if I'd never got involved.'

His lips clamped for a full minute, the tension grew in that tiny room. Then he said in a tone that was all the more dangerous because it was soft, 'You don't mean that, Jancy, but if you can't find it in your heart to forgive me then do me one favour.'

She eyed him suspiciously. 'And what is that?'

'Don't marry Giles.' His voice was choked with emotion.

There was no doubting his sincerity and she almost weakened, then she remembered what he had done to her. 'You no longer have any influence over me,' she snapped coldly. 'I'll do whatever I please.'

'It will be a mistake.'

'My mistake was falling in love with you in the first place,' she thrust aggressively. 'It's one I shall never forget.'

Saxon poured himself another drink, looked at her enquiringly. 'Would you like one?'

She shook her head. 'All I'd like to do is get out of here.'

'Dammit, Jancy,' he grated savagely. 'I'm not going to let you go. You're my woman. You belong to me. You shall not marry Giles. I forbid it.'

Jancy experienced a strange thrill at the strong tones in his voice. But she lifted her chin and met his eyes bravely. 'How will you stop me?'

His smile was confident. 'I shan't give you a moment's peace. I shall keep on at you until you come to your senses. And if Giles sees us together then so be it. He knows how I feel about you.'

Jancy had never been more aware of his indomitable strength. It was reflected in the rigid lines of his body, the aggressive thrust of his jaw, the sheer arrogant maleness of him. Her heart throbbed and she felt as though a whole brass band was playing inside her chest.

'Just as soon as this cruise is over, Jancy, we're getting married, make no mistake about that.'

A ripple of shock ran through her. 'You can't mean that? You can't make me.'

'Can't I?' His lip curled. 'There's not much in this life I can't do. I want you and I'm going to have you. You have no say in the matter.'

Jancy found it painful to breathe. 'But why? Why would you want to marry a woman who doesn't love you?'

His mouth firmed. 'You won't hate me for long,

I promise you that. The physical attraction is still there, as you freely admit. We'd soon stop fighting and become the intimate friends we once were. There's nothing I wouldn't do for you, Jancy. I want your happiness above all else.'

'In that case,' she thrust bitterly, 'get out of my hair. I'd never be happy with you, not after the way you treated me.'

He shook his head angrily. 'So far as I'm concerned our parting has merely strengthened my feelings. Once we're married you'll realise it is the best thing that's ever happened to you.'

He produced a bottle of champagne, popping the cork, pouring the sparkling liquid into two glasses. 'To our future happiness.'

'To your downfall,' grated Jancy, sipping the wine, wrinkling her nose as the bubbles went up it.

Her words angered him. It was clear in his eyes. But he smiled pleasantly. 'I know you don't mean that.'

'I mean it more than I've ever meant anything in my life,' said Jancy, finishing the rest of the champagne and putting down her glass, hoping that now she could make her escape.

But he filled it up again. 'Don't rush away, Jancy. Stay and talk, at least.'

His tone was persuasive and against her better judgement she sat down. He told her about his previous trip—his first—on the *Ocean Queen*. She wanted to ask what had made him take this job but was afraid her interest might be misconstrued.

They finished the bottle of champagne and Jancy felt some of their old rapport return, but knowing that this was what Saxon intended she was careful not to appear too friendly.

When he pulled her into his arms, though, and

kissed her, she responded without hesitation, clinging to him as she had so many times in the past, returning his kisses unashamedly. Whether it was the effect of the champagne or whether it was the drugging influence of his presence, Jancy did not know. Perhaps it was a mixture of both. She had known, almost from the moment she entered his room, that it would be inevitable.

There was triumph on his face when he finally let her go, and neither spoke as she hurried from the cabin. Her face flaming she took a walk on the upper deck, needing time to clear her head before she checked on her employer. It had been insane letting Saxon kiss her after the way she had denied herself to him earlier. How good he must be feeling.

When she eventually returned to her cabin it was empty. It occurred to her that Mrs Fairfax and the admiral were probably lunching. She had given no thought to the time—nor indeed was she hungry.

She wandered aimlessly about the ship, playing a game of table tennis with one of the few remaining souls on board, taking a leisurely swim, and when she checked her room again Mrs Fairfax was there.

Surprisingly she looked a picture of health, no sign of her languor remaining, her face a healthy pink. 'You're never going to believe this,' she said to Jancy at once. 'Jacob's asked me to marry him.'

Jancy gasped, her eyes widening. 'But that's wonderful.'

'Yes,' said the woman, wringing her hands, unable to sit still for one minute. 'It was love at first sight. I expect you think that's stupid at our age. But, well, it's a different sort of love from when you're young. We're both old enough to know what to look for in a partner and I know I've found it in Jacob.'

'Then I wish you both every happiness in the world,' said Jancy. It looked as though Giles' mocking suggestion that they have a double wedding might come true after all.

The dining room was partly empty that evening. Some of those who had gone ashore had returned but most were still absent. Giles was one of the missing ones.

Saxon was already at the table and she felt the power of him as she crossed the floor. She kept a pace or two behind Mrs Fairfax as the woman sailed majestically towards her loved one who was deep in conversation with the surgeon.

They both stood as the two women approached. Saxon held out his hand. 'I believe congratulations are in order?'

'I'm so happy,' said Fiona Fairfax. 'And to think if you hadn't suggested we sit at your table we might never have met. I'm deeply indebted.'

As there was only the four of them that evening there was no opportunity for Saxon to involve Jancy in private conversation, but she was still thankful when the meal was over and she could make her escape.

She went to bed early, scorning the entertainment provided, pretending to be asleep when Mrs Fairfax eventually came back.

The next morning at breakfast Giles was full of all he had seen and done the day before and it was some little time before he mentioned his mother's engagement.

'I'm really glad for her,' he said. 'She has such a big capacity for loving it's about time she was on the receiving end. I trust your day wasn't too boring? From what I can gather my mother spent most of her time with the admiral?'

'That's right,' admitted Jancy. 'I could have come with you. I wish I had.'

'Did Saxon make a nuisance of himself?' His voice was suspicious.

She nodded. It would be pointless denying it.

'I hope you told him where to get off? Would you like me to have another word with him? It will be a pleasure to stick my fist in his face. He certainly won't take me by surprise a second time.'

'I don't think it will come to that,' she said. 'I can handle Saxon. I've made it very clear I'm no longer interested.'

He looked sceptical. 'You never told me exactly why you two broke up. What did he do to make you so bitter?'

Jancy shrugged. 'It's too ridiculous to go into detail, but someone told him I'd deliberately set out to make him notice me, that I'd won a bet because of it. He wouldn't listen to my side of the story, he thought I'd made a fool of him. He's apparently realised he's made a mistake and wants to start again, but how do you trust a guy like that?'

'You don't,' said Giles. 'You're doing the right thing if you ask me—but then I'm biased.' He gave a weak grin. 'How about a game of tennis?'

Checking on his mother later Jancy found her up and dressed but still in her cabin. 'I'm following doctor's orders and taking it easy. Jacob's borrowed a good book from the library and says it will keep him happy until lunchtime. He's almost as bad as the doctor,' she grumbled good-naturedly.

'I'll keep you company,' said Jancy.

Mrs Fairfax shook her head. 'I wouldn't dream of it. You go and enjoy yourself.'

But Jancy insisted. 'I've just finished an energetic game of tennis with your son, I could do with a rest. You know what a demanding player he is.'

'I'm sorry you missed your chance to see Antigua with him yesterday. I was unaware that he'd gone alone until the doctor mentioned it. Did he get his medical supplies?'

The sudden question took Jancy by surprise. If she admitted they hadn't gone Mrs Fairfax would want to know the whole story, after the fuss Saxon had made about needing two signatures, so she nodded and quickly changed the subject. 'What sort of a wedding are you going to have? Will it be soon? I don't suppose you'll want to wait.'

'I'd really like to get married in church,' she said. 'A big swanky do. I fancy a cream lace suit and exotic orchids—but Jacob wants something quiet. A registry office, he said.' She wrinkled her nose in distaste. 'With just a couple of close friends. I think he's shy. You wouldn't expect that, with a man of his type, would you?'

'A lot of men are when it comes to getting married,' said Jancy. 'But don't give in. It is after all a woman's big day. Why shouldn't you have your own way?'

'I hope that when you and Giles——' Mrs Fairfax stopped abruptly. 'There I go, jumping the gun. I'm sorry, Jancy, but you're so right for him. I'd really like to see you two make a go of it.'

Jancy almost told Mrs Fairfax about their engagement then, but something held her back. She had promised to marry Giles for all the wrong reasons, and although she was not planning to back out she would rather wait until the cruise was over and Saxon out of her hair before committing herself by telling his mother. 'What is to be will be,' she murmured. 'How about a cup of tea? Shall I ring for some?'

The crisis passed but Jancy did not feel entirely comfortable in her employer's presence after that. It was a relief when Jacob collected Fiona for lunch and she joined Giles on the upper deck.

'Your mother's been hinting that she would like me to marry you,' she said.

Giles smiled broadly. 'I hope you told her about our engagement? It's about time she knew.'

'No, I'm afraid I didn't,' she admitted apologetically. 'I was worried about taking the edge off her own happiness. I think we ought to wait until after the cruise.'

He shook his head, lips compressed sadly. 'I have a feeling you don't want to marry me at all. I think Saxon means more to you than you're admitting. You are right, we should wait. We'll see how things are when we get back.'

He attempted to keep his voice light but did not succeed. Jancy understood his feelings and sympathised, but did not know what she could do about it.

She spent the rest of the afternoon sunning herself and attending a port talk with Giles on Martinique. They were calling at this island tomorrow and it would be one of the longest stopping places yet. Sixteen and a half hours in which to explore. Jancy knew that Giles was anxious to see all he could.

'I hope you'll come with me,' he said.

Jancy shook her head. 'I'm quite sure the doctor won't allow your mother to go ashore. I must stay with her. I know I shall probably not be needed, but it is after all the job I'm supposed to be doing.'

He looked sad. 'I thought as much. Just mind you keep out of Saxon Marriot's way. It's a pity about my mother but I'm determined not to let her illness spoil things. I'll find someone else to accompany me. It's not much fun on your own.'

All too soon it was time for dinner. It was the one part of each day that Jancy dreaded. But she need not have feared. Debra Forrester had already seated herself at Saxon's side.

She did not know whether sitting opposite Saxon was worse than sitting beside him. Each time she looked up his eyes were upon her. She made a pretence of talking animatedly to Giles but knew she was not fooling the surgeon.

The next morning Mrs Fairfax asked Jancy to accompany her to the doctor's consulting room. 'I want to ask him if I can go ashore. I feel one hundred per cent fit today.'

Saxon examined her and grudgingly gave his approval. 'But no overdoing it,' he warned. 'I've already had a word in the admiral's ear. No rushing about like a young thing, do you hear?'

Mrs Fairfax smiled. 'Anything you say, doctor. I feel so alive this morning. I feel about sixteen again. Isn't it wonderful to be in love?'

Saxon glanced from her to Jancy who was hovering behind. 'It is indeed,' he said positively, and only Jancy knew his words held a double meaning.

'Of course I'll take Jancy along with me,' said Fiona Fairfax.

'I don't think that will be necessary,' said Saxon, much to Jancy's dismay. 'Not with the admiral keeping his eye on you.'

The older woman beamed her pleasure. 'Then you'll be able to enjoy yourself with Giles, my dear. I'm sure you'll have much more fun with him than in the company of a couple of old fogies like us.'

'Giles has already left,' said Jancy. 'You were asleep and he didn't want to disturb you. I thought you'd be spending the day here and I'd be needed.'

Mrs Fairfax looked troubled. 'But you can't stay on board, and I wouldn't dream of letting you go off alone. You'll have to come with us.'

'It will be my pleasure to take Jancy ashore,' said Saxon, awarding the older woman one of his special smiles which almost always assured he got his own way. 'I intend doing a spot of sight-seeing myself and it's very rare I have the company of a beautiful lady.'

Jancy could not believe that Mrs Fairfax would be taken in, but indeed her employer smiled warmly. 'How very kind of you, I'm sure Jancy will enjoy that.'

'I shall look after her most carefully,' he assured, and to Jancy, 'I'll see you later, then. I must clear up here first.'

Back in their cabin Mrs Fairfax said, 'I do hope you have wonderful day, Jancy. I'm sorry it's not Giles you're going with. I wish you'd woken me, I could have told him it was all right.'

'Don't worry,' said Jancy. 'I'm quite looking forward to going with the surgeon.' God, what a lie that was. Spending the day with Saxon Marriot was the last thing she wanted.

CHAPTER SIX

I<small>T</small> was with reluctance that Jancy finally accompanied Saxon from the ship, making no attempt to hide her displeasure.

When they were in the hired car she felt even worse. She had forgotten how overpowering he could be. The car was so small he filled it with his presence, expanding into every corner so that there was no escape.

Deliberately she stared out of the window, realising for herself why this island was sometimes called the Island of Flowers. They were everywhere; hibiscus, bougainvillaea, wild orchids, a maze of tropical blooms.

She envied Saxon his new job, seeing all these exciting places. It must be so much more enjoyable than working in a hospital. But for her this was a once-in-a-lifetime holiday, and even though she did not want to be with Saxon saw no point in ruining her day. She might never get another chance to visit this Caribbean island.

He reached out and touched her hand. 'I can't tell you how much this means to me. It's been too long since we spent any length of time together.'

Jancy bit back a sharp retort. What point was there in antagonising him? But it did not stop her from feeling bitter. He had deliberately blackmailed her into this unfortunate situation. Despite her animosity, though, her chemical reaction had not lessened. His hand on hers had been brief, almost impersonal, yet it had affected her as much as if he had kissed her.

She could still feel the imprint of it, as though he had burnt into her flesh. She looked down, stupidly expecting to see a red mark, but there was nothing. It was all in her mind.

She was glad when he suddenly distracted her attention, pointing out a two-headed coconut palm and a line of colourful native fishing boats which had been carved from gum trees.

But it was the ruined town of Saint Pierre that fired her imagination. 'It was once called the Paris of the West Indies,' Saxon informed. 'Unfortunately, the whole city was destroyed when Mount Pelée erupted at the beginning of the twentieth century. The explosion set off an avalanche of incandescent gas and ash that swept down the slopes annihilating everything in its path. The only survivor was a prisoner in an underground jail. There's irony for you.'

As they scrambled over ruins now practically hidden by tangled tropical growth Jancy tried to imagine what it once looked like. There were new houses rising from the devastation, but not until he took her inside the museum and she saw pictures of the city as it once was with its magnificent cathedral and theatre, did she realise they would never recapture its former glory.

'I can't understand them rebuilding,' she whispered, half scared. 'What if it erupts again?'

'Some say it's burnt itself out,' said Saxon, 'but I think I agree with you. It's somewhat risky. If I wanted to live in this area I'd opt for Basse-Terre on the other side of Mount Pelée.'

'But aren't they in as much danger?'

He smiled and shook his head. 'If what I've

been told is correct it's now been realised that volcanoes are slightly tilted and only ever erupt from one side. Basse-Terre is perfectly safe.'

'Even so,' said Jancy, pulling a wry face, 'I don't think I'd risk it.'

It certainly gave her food for thought and she was silent as they continued their journey. But it was a companionable silence. Quite what she had been expecting today she was not sure, but Saxon was certainly setting himself out to be a perfect companion.

It was pleasant sitting in the open air restaurant in the middle of a banana plantation and Jancy tried *kalalou*, a subtle and savoury French Creole herb soup, followed by stuffed crab which she pronounced absolutely delicious.

Saxon ordered a jug of La Punch Martinique. 'It's the island's favourite drink,' he informed. 'It's a mixture of sugar syrup, lime, ice and rum.'

All day Jancy expected him to make some reference to Giles, was surprised and pleased when he did not. She could almost imagine they were back in the old days, that there had never been any rift between them. How wonderful a holiday in these idyllic islands would have been under those circumstances.

Their day ended in Fort de France, the island's capital. There were gendarmes everywhere, cafés and bistros, and hundreds of souvenir shops. Jancy purchased a carved figurine for her sister, Kate.

While admiring the realistic white marble effigy of the Empress Josephine Jancy lost Saxon, but he appeared a few minutes later and ushered her into a corner. From his pocket he took a tiny leather box, opening it to reveal an exquisite emerald and diamond engagement ring.

'What's that for?' Jancy demanded, her stomach contracting painfully. It was not difficult to guess what he had in mind.

He took her hand and Jancy watched in fascinated horror as he slid it on to her finger. His touch caused a tremor of pure unadulterated desire, and she knew that whatever the circumstances he would always have this power over her. She was a fool, allowing him to disturb her like this, but it was an emotion over which she had no control. There was a satisfied smile on his face as he withdrew the ring, putting it safely back into its box.

With its disappearance Jancy snapped out of her stupor. 'You don't honestly think I'll ever give up Giles for you?'

'I don't think. I know,' he said grimly. 'And I intend being prepared.'

'You're insane!' she declared.

'Not insane, determined.'

She shook her head and turned away. How was she ever going to get through to him?

'I think,' he said, 'we ought to make our way back to the ship. The *Grand Ballets De La Martinique* are coming to entertain us. We mustn't miss them. They regularly perform traditional dances on the island as well as in Europe and the States. They're very good. I shall look forward to dancing the beguine with you tonight.'

Jancy was more than willing to return, she had had enough of her day out. He had quite ruined it by this last unexpected purchase, proving without a doubt that his intentions were serious, that he would not give up until he had won her back from Giles.

Once on board he said, 'I expect you'll want to take a rest and freshen up. I'll see you at dinner.'

He took her face between his hands, looking deeply into her eyes, searching for goodness knows what before kissing her lips lightly. 'You're mine,' he said, so faintly she hardly heard, then briskly walked away.

Even that brief kiss violated her senses and Jancy knew that it would be the easiest thing in the world to give in to him. But for her own long-lasting peace of mind she dare not. She must keep him at arm's length. Allowing herself to be drawn into potentially dangerous situations, such as today, was asking for trouble of the worst kind.

Mrs Fairfax had already returned and looked at Jancy questioningly as she entered the cabin. 'Have you had a good day?'

The woman's voice did not hold its usual sincerity and Jancy wondered whether she was not well. 'Quite pleasant, but how about you? I didn't expect you back yet.'

'My day was ruined.'

Jancy looked at her sharply. Fiona Fairfax did look pale, certainly not so animated as she had that morning. 'You did too much? I should have known better than to let you go alone. I wish I'd come.'

'So do I,' snapped her employer. 'We met Giles on the island.' It was an accusation and her eyes flicked coldly over the young girl. 'Apparently you've been deceiving me. Saxon Marriot is the man you were running away from when you applied for the job as my nurse. Is that right?'

Jancy silently cursed Giles. 'I'm afraid so.'

'I thought you said he was no longer interested?' The woman's lips were pursed tightly.

'He wasn't,' said Jancy, 'but he's since found out something that's made him change his mind.'

'And now he wants to marry you?' The woman's blue eyes were like steel, fixed unblinkingly on her nurse.

Jancy nodded. 'The feeling's not mutual, though. I could never trust him. It will be a relief when this voyage is over. I never wish to see him again.'

Mrs Fairfax tossed her head disbelievingly. 'Giles was very upset when I told him you'd gone off with Saxon. He seemed to think you were in danger. Naturally, if I'd known about your earlier relationship I would never have allowed it. It was all I could do to stop Giles rushing all over the island trying to find you.'

'He should know that I'm capable of taking care of myself where Saxon's concerned.'

'From what I can make out,' returned her employer, 'Saxon is a very determined man. Giles told me about the fight they'd had. He also told me that you and he are engaged. That's something else I wish to discuss. Why did you insist on keeping it secret? You know it's what I want.'

Jancy swallowed uncomfortably. How could she tell Mrs Fairfax that it was because she was not sure the engagement would last? That although she had promised Giles she would marry him it was still Saxon she loved?

Mrs Fairfax had only her son's interests at heart. Whatever Jancy said would make no difference. But Jancy knew she had to try and soothe the woman. If she carried on in this way there was a very real danger of her suffering a heart attack. Already her colour was too high for Jancy's liking.

'Mrs Fairfax,' she said, 'I'm sure Giles has alarmed you unnecessarily.'

'Giles has not alarmed me,' came the strong reply. 'It's my son who's distressed.'

'But I've done nothing wrong,' cried Jancy. 'I've spent the day with an ex-boyfriend, admittedly, but it doesn't mean anything. It hasn't made me feel any differently towards Saxon. He let me down twice. I have no intention of giving him another opportunity. I went with him because I wanted to see Martinique.'

'You could have come with us.' Mrs Fairfax's face was twisted with emotion.

'I was quite prepared to do that,' said Jancy. 'But you yourself suggested I might be better off with Saxon.'

The woman's lips thinned. 'That was before I knew how well you were acquainted. I'm very disappointed in you, Jancy. I really thought you were a girl of integrity, that I could trust you.'

Jancy bit her lip anxiously. 'I'm sorry you feel that way—but I can only say again that I've done nothing wrong. I'm not ashamed of going out with Saxon Marriot today. I can still hold my head high. Giles has no reason to be jealous.'

'Let's hope he'll see it that way,' said his mother thickly. 'Go to him now, he's in his cabin.'

Jancy turned reluctantly, and with her heart as heavy as a stone crossed the corridor and tapped on his door. He opened it but swung away uninterestedly when he saw it was Jancy.

She followed him inside. 'Giles,' she said at once. 'It's not what you think.' It pained her to see him upset.

'Then what is it like? You tell me.' He turned on her savagely, and she was shocked by the despair in his eyes. They were ringed with red and he looked like a man who had been through hell. 'If you hate the guy as much as you profess then I can't see why you would willingly spend a day with him.'

'It was not my idea,' said Jancy.

'You could have refused.'

'Then your mother would have wondered why. She was all for it. It would have meant explanations. Although now, thanks to you, she's found out anyway.'

'I had to tell her,' he said. 'I couldn't believe it when I heard you'd gone off with him.'

'But did you have to let her see you were worried?'

He sighed. 'Doesn't every parent know the moods of their children? I couldn't pull the wool over her eyes.'

'And now what?' asked Jancy sadly. 'I can assure you that I've not changed my mind about Saxon. Today has made no difference.'

He looked at her scornfully. 'Don't tell me he didn't make a pass? You're forgetting I know exactly how he feels.'

'Well he didn't,' snapped Jancy. 'He was a perfect gentleman.' She dared not tell him about the ring. It was ironical that the man she was supposed to be engaged to had not yet bought her one, while the man she professed to despise had one ready in his pocket.

'I'd like to believe you, Jancy, really I would, but——' He paused and looked at her painfully. 'I can't go on with this engagement, not if you're going to keep seeing Saxon.'

'I can't avoid it,' she said. 'How can you not see anyone on this ship?'

'I realise you'll have contact with him professionally,' replied Giles, 'but it need go no further.'

'It's what I'd like myself,' said Jancy, 'but you know how stubborn Saxon is.'

He looked at her impatiently. 'You can't have the best of both worlds. It's either Saxon or me. You must make your decision.'

Jancy swallowed and stood looking at him, not knowing what to say. Giles had been her buffer against Saxon. In her heart of hearts she had known she would never marry him. But neither could she marry Saxon.

She would never know when he was going to accuse her of something else. She would be on tenterhooks all the time, living on her nerves, and in the end it might be her own inability to accept the situation that would be her downfall.

But there was still Giles. How could she tell him that she did not love him, that she never had? What a difficult situation she had got herself in to.

When he next spoke he sounded resigned. 'Your indecision has given me your answer. I should never have asked you to marry me. Saxon forced my hand, I suppose. If I'd waited until after the voyage it might have worked. In a way I'm as much to blame. I tried to press you into something for which you were not ready.'

Jancy looked at him sadly. 'What can I say?'

'It's best you say nothing.'

'What are we going to tell your mother? She's very cross with me. It's going to make the rest of the cruise unbearable.'

'You should have thought of that before you went off with Saxon,' he thrust bitterly.

'Can't we still—er, pretend that we're going to get married?' Jancy gnawed her lower lip as she waited for his reply. It was a big thing she was asking of him, unfair too. She had no right even suggesting it. Hadn't she hurt him enough?

'You really think my mother would accept that—after the way I reacted this afternoon?'

Jancy shrugged. 'I assured her it meant nothing—me going off with Saxon. She might believe us.'

'And pigs might fly,' he flung incautiously. 'It's a ridiculous suggestion. You don't know what you're asking.'

'I do know,' said Jancy miserably. 'And I have no right, but can't you see it from my point of view, too? Don't you care how I feel?'

'Of course I care.' He came across and took her hands. 'I love you, Jancy, that's why I'm mad with you. I'm as jealous as hell of Saxon Marriot. It's as clear as the nose on your face that you prefer him to me.'

Jancy felt shocked. 'I don't see how you can say that. What we once had going for us is over. I wouldn't have him if he was handed to me on a gold plate. Marriage between me and Saxon would never work. I'm grateful I found out in time.'

'It's yourself you're trying to convince,' he said sadly. 'You love him. You keep telling yourself you don't, but you do.'

She eyed him worriedly. 'How can you say that?'

'Because *I* love *you*. I'm attuned to your every mood. I've seen the way you look at him in your unguarded moments. I've watched you at the dining table. You come alive when he talks to you, and when he touches you, well, it's as though he's making love to you. Do you deny it?'

Jancy closed her eyes, shame filling her. It was true, all true. She had never realised how perceptive Giles was. He must love her very much. And all she had been doing was using him! He ought to hate her now, instead of still loving her.

When he pulled her against him her tears began to flow. He was very patient, even pushing his handkerchief into her hands. But she could feel the tenseness in him and knew that he felt awkward in this situation.

She swallowed and looked at him sadly, seeing his face through a mist of tears. He looked ready to cry himself. 'I'm sorry, Giles,' she said. 'I never intended you to know.'

'Just as you never intended to marry me!' His voice was thick with an emotion he was too proud to release, the accusation stabbing her all the same.

Jancy looked down at the handkerchief, twisting it between her fingers. 'How can you ever forgive me?'

'Because I'm a fool. Because I love you. Because I want your happiness.'

Jancy's tears began again and this time she made no attempt to restrain them. 'You're a good man, Giles. I hope one day you'll find someone worthy of your love. I wouldn't blame you if you never spoke to me again.'

He heaved a sigh and seemed to take a firm hold of himself. 'I have my mother to consider. She's relied on me since my father died. I love her very much, it upsets me to see her ill. I feared for her this afternoon.'

'I know,' said Jancy. 'She worries me too. I'm afraid she might have another heart attack if she carries on this way.'

'Then I suggest,' he said quietly, unhappily, 'that we keep up our farcical engagement—until she's happily married to her admiral. The shock won't hit her so badly then. Jacob will console her. In fact I might let him into our secret.'

'She might not feel I'm good enough for you, now she's found out about me and Saxon. She did not like to think I'd deceived her. Not that I had anything to hide, I simply did not think it necessary to tell her. I never thought he'd behave the way he has.'

'You leave Mother to me,' he said. 'I'll go and see her now. Get yourself a drink, you look as though you need it.'

Jancy was glad to escape, but did not go to any of the bars. Instead she went up on deck, inhaling the sultry evening air. The beaches of Martinique were deserted at this hour. The island with its backdrop of tropical forests and volcanic mountains looked serene. But she would never again hear its name without remembering this day.

When finally she returned to her cabin it was empty. Her relief knew no bounds. She did not feel up to another emotional scene and hoped Giles had managed to convince his mother that her going out with Saxon today made no difference to their feelings for each other. Mrs Fairfax's health was important to them both.

When she walked into the restaurant later congratulations were thrown at her from all sides. She had not realised the news would spread so quickly. She slid on to her seat beside Giles and he kissed her warmly.

Saxon's eyes shot daggers from the other side of the table, although he too added his congratulations.

'Two engagements in one family,' said Debra Forrester brightly. 'Is it going to be a double wedding?'

Jancy was sick of hearing about double weddings, but somehow managed to fix a smile to her face, glancing at Giles, leaving him to give the answer.

But Mrs Fairfax spoke up for them. 'Of course not. I can't have a pretty young girl like Jancy ruining my day. She'd quite take the limelight off me.' There was general laughter. 'Besides, we shall have two excuses for celebrations.'

Jancy wondered whether Giles had truly been able to reassure his mother, or whether the woman had her suspicions and this was a way of getting round it. When she caught Mrs Fairfax's eye, though, her employer's smile was sincere enough.

'I never realised it would be this difficult.' Giles' soft voice reached her ear.

'At least it's made your mother happy,' she said, 'and that's what it's all about.'

Somehow Jancy managed to get through the rest of the meal without giving away the fact that she was not the deliriously happy girl she purported to be. Debra Forrester claimed Saxon's attention and he did not seem unhappy with the situation, although more than once Jancy found his eyes upon her, an enigmatic expression in their depths.

Giles too noticed and Jancy saw his lips tighten in disapproval, but he said nothing, putting on an act which convinced everyone around the table.

Jancy wondered how long it would be before Saxon cornered her. He was probably thinking that the announcement had been made for his benefit, not realising that it was Mrs Fairfax they were trying to convince.

After dinner they gathered in the Flamingo lounge to watch the *Ballets De La Martinique*.

They were a flamboyant group performing all sorts of dances that Jancy had never seen before and for a while she actually managed to forget her troubles.

Nor did Saxon come to claim his beguine. In fact he was nowhere in sight, which surprised her, because he had made a point of saying that this group was too good to miss.

When she eventually returned to her cabin Mrs Fairfax was in bed, though not asleep, calling Jancy to her side. 'I think Giles is being very forgiving. I sincerely hope that you will give him no further cause for distrust.'

Jancy winced inwardly, managing a smile. 'I'll try not to, Mrs Fairfax.'

'He loves you very much, and despite what happened I, too, think you will make him a good wife. I like you, Jancy. It hurt me to think you had been deceiving me, but Giles explained that it was really none of our business. What happened before you met us is over and done with. I just hope you don't let the past intrude into the present. I should hate him to be hurt.'

'Rest assured I shall not hurt your son,' said Jancy sincerely. 'We understand each other now.'

'I'm glad.' The woman looked content as she slid down between the sheets. 'It's been an exhausting day, Jancy, I'm tired. Good night, my dear.'

'Good night, Mrs Fairfax.' Jancy stood looking down at her employer for a moment or two after the woman had closed her eyes. Impulsively she bent over and pressed a kiss to her brow. The woman smiled and Jancy tiptoed out of the room.

She did not close the door between them in case Mrs Fairfax called out to her in the night. Not that she ever did, but with today's upset Jancy could not be sure.

When she climbed into bed herself she found it impossible to sleep. So much was on her mind, so much had happened. She wondered exactly what Saxon was thinking now. He must be very sure of her to have bought that ring—and yet only hours afterwards the public announcement had been made of her engagement to Giles.

Had it hurt him? she wondered, feeling a grim pleasure. He was so sure he would get her to change her mind that it served him right to have his plans explode in his face.

She was more concerned for Giles. She had hurt him more deeply than she intended, not realising how much he loved her. He was certainly proving himself a very caring sort of person. Not many men would put their mother's happiness before their own.

During the night the *Ocean Queen* steamed towards Trinidad and Tobago and the throb of the engines lulled Jancy to sleep. She tried to avoid Saxon for the next day, but knew she would not manage it for ever.

The weather changed abruptly, a storm blew up out of nowhere. The ship heaved and rolled. If it hadn't been frightening it would have been fascinating watching the water cover the windows, first to starboard and then to port.

The captain made continual announcements over the public address system, reassuring the passengers that it was a temporary tropical storm and nothing out of the ordinary.

Jancy knew she had not been alone in thinking that the whole of this cruise would be sunny and calm. It had caught everyone by surprise. The storm lasted for no more than an hour but in that short time it wreaked havoc. The whole of the luncheon buffet, so carefully prepared and presented, slid off the table. Furniture rolled across rooms and decks.

Jancy returned to her cabin to find Mrs Fairfax clinging to her bunk, the whole room in chaos. She made the older woman sit down and they remained there until the storm had blown itself out.

Fiona Fairfax looked dreadfully ill and Jancy knew she ought to summon the doctor. But he would be so busy. She had seen people caught unawares and flung across the deck. There were sure to be injuries. In fact she wondered whether she ought to volunteer to help in the hospital.

But of course Mrs Fairfax was her main concern. Jancy insisted she take one of her tablets and get into bed. Gradually some colour returned to her cheeks. The admiral came along shortly afterwards and Jancy was able to leave her for a while, knowing that if she was needed he would fetch her.

She made her way below to the hospital and saw that her fears were confirmed. There was a whole queue of people waiting to have cuts bandaged, although so far as she could see at a quick glance there was nothing seriously wrong with any of them.

The nurses were working flat out and were relieved to have extra help. When the room was finally cleared Saxon turned to Jancy and thanked her.

'Don't thank me,' she said. 'It's what I'm trained for. Anyone would have done the same.'

'Would they?' They were alone in his consulting

room, Saxon sitting at his desk, Jancy standing beside him, and there was no fear that they would be overheard. 'Not the way you feel about me, Jancy. You made your point very clear when you announced your engagement. Was that Giles' idea or yours? You'd kept it remarkably quiet up till then. I can only assume that me buying that ring made you behave as you did?'

'You should never have bought it,' said Jancy. 'You wasted your money.'

His eyes narrowed. 'I think not. You'll never go through with it.'

Jancy wondered whether he realised that by constantly pressurising her he was sending her further and further away. 'You're so sure,' she said distantly. 'Aren't you used to taking no for an answer?'

'Don't fool yourself that you're being virtuous,' he snarled. 'If you've forgotten that first day we met, I haven't.'

'You think I'd forget what you called me then?' Jancy's green eyes were wide. 'Or your further accusations—all without proof? It's something that will remain with me for the rest of my life. Giles would never condemn me without a fair hearing. You'd do as well to take a leaf out of his book.'

His face hardened. 'I fail to see what that man has going for him. I refuse to accept that you prefer him to me.' He caught her wrist in a biting grip which she felt sure would snap her bones. 'I'm not going to let you ruin your life, Jancy. Keep up your little game if you wish, until this cruise is over, but believe me you won't get away with it for ever.'

'You can't force me to marry you, Saxon.'

'Can't I?'

'Only a fool would marry a man who's away so much. Being a doctor's wife is bad enough at the best of times, but married to someone who's away for the biggest part of the year is not exactly my idea of fun.'

'Didn't I tell you?' He caught her other wrist and pulled her down so that her eyes were on a level with his. 'I'm filling in for a colleague of mine, that's all. I'm opening my own clinic. It should be ready when I get back. You'll be the wife of a very rich man, Jancy. I shall have a team of doctors working under me and if all goes to plan I shall have plenty of leisure time to spend with you.'

'You're talking as though our marriage is cut and dried.' She was surprised by this information, but it made no difference. He was still the same man who had cast her aside as inconsequentially as one might a pair of old shoes.

'So far as I'm concerned, it is,' he said. 'Although I think it might be necessary to have another word with our friend, Giles.'

Jancy's head jerked and she tried to free herself, all to no avail. His grip was tighter than an iron band.

'I'll wait, though, until we're back in England. I don't want to upset his dear mother. She thinks a lot of you, Jancy.'

'She did do,' she snapped bitterly, 'until she discovered that you and I had once been very close.'

'You finally told her?'

'Not me, Giles. When we were on Martinique his mother found him wandering about on his own. He was—upset—when he discovered I was sight-seeing with you.'

'Methinks the man really loves you,' mocked
Saxon.

'He does,' retorted Jancy, 'and I'd thank you to
leave us alone.' She hoped she sounded convincing.
It was getting harder and harder to repudiate him.
'Let me go, Saxon. I need to check on Mrs
Fairfax. The storm upset her. I've left her in bed.'

'Then I'll come with you,' he said at once, much to
her dismay. 'According to the captain we don't
encounter these storms often but when we do they
can be pretty horrendous. I've given out more
tablets for sea-sickness than anything else, and that's
pretty unusual when a ship's as well stablised as this
one. If you escaped you're one of the lucky ones.'

When they reached the cabin Mrs Fairfax
looked suspiciously at Jancy, as if wondering
whether she hadn't had some secret assignation
with Saxon. But Saxon was at his most professional
and immediately allayed her fears, treating Jancy
as if she were no different from any of the other
nurses. Apart from rapping out an instruction he
did not even look at her again before leaving.

'I'm glad to see the two of you are being
sensible,' said Mrs Fairfax.

'I told you it was all over,' replied Jancy.

Her employer heaved a sigh of relief. 'Perhaps
we can now settle down to a restful few days.'

Which was all that remained of the cruise! Jancy
was amazed how quickly time had passed.

But it was inevitable that she and Saxon should
meet and she knew that on each occasion he would
take the opportunity to warn her that her reprieve
was temporary. Nevertheless Jancy was determined
not to let him ruin the rest of her holiday. She
clung to Giles as much as possible and he valiantly
behaved as though there was nothing wrong.

In one way it was easy for him to act naturally, thought Jancy, to bestow on her all the love and affection that he felt, but it must be heartbreaking too, knowing she returned none of his feelings. She, therefore, went out of her way to be extra nice.

The evening of the ninth day at sea a fancy dress ball was announced and they spent a lot of time planning what to wear. 'I think,' said Giles thoughtfully, 'that we ought to go as a pair then Saxon will have no opportunity to single you out.'

'Good idea,' replied Jancy. 'How about Harlequin and Columbine?'

'Or Romeo and Juliet?' he suggested darkly.

He sounded serious and Jancy laughed nervously. 'Perhaps Laurel and Hardy? I'm sure the admiral would lend you one of his suits to pad out.'

'And how about you, Mother?' asked Giles.

'Oh, I'm too old for such nonsense,' she said.

'No, you're not,' put in Jacob. 'You'd make a very good Queen Victoria, but I don't think I look very much like Albert. Perhaps Henry VIII?' He chuckled. 'I could enlist some of the single women as my wives.'

'Oh, no you don't,' said Mrs Fairfax, but she laughed all the same, and grudgingly agreed to enter into the spirit of the evening.

During the next day, while they sailed from Trinidad to Curacao, Jancy helped Mrs Fairfax alter one of her dresses and spent a lot of time adapting her own and Giles' clothes to suit their chosen parts, having finally decided to go as Robin Hood and Maid Marion.

There was an air of expectation over the passengers on the day of the ball and after dinner,

when it was time to get into their costumes, Jancy
felt a bubbling excitement.

The ballroom was filled to capacity and despite
the fact that Giles had thought they would remain
inseparable, Jancy found herself whisked away by
Napoleon, a very creditable skeleton, and even
Winston Churchill.

She lost Giles altogether. Mrs Fairfax waltzed
by on the arm of Henry VIII. At least she had kept
her man, thought Jancy. And then in the dim light
of the room she saw Giles weaving his way
towards her, his feathered hat, a trifle too big,
sitting on his ears, his mask effectively concealing
his true identity.

'Where did you get to?' she laughed, breathlessly
flinging herself at him. 'I thought the idea was to
stick together? It's been over an hour. I was
beginning to panic.'

'In case you bumped into me?' Familiar blue
eyes glinted from the slits in the mask. Too late
Jancy realised her mistake.

CHAPTER SEVEN

'WHAT are you doing, dressed like that?' demanded Jancy icily.

Saxon's mouth widened into a wicked smile.

'There's no law says I can't.'

'You've done it deliberately! You somehow found out what Giles was going to wear and chose the same, hoping I'd confuse the two of you.' Had she looked at him more closely she would never have done so. There was his hair for one thing; although he had done his best to hide it, it still curled darkly from beneath the hat, and those sensual lips could never belong to Giles. Saxon had obviously counted on the fact that they were a similar build and relied on the diffused lighting to do the rest.

His arms tigthened about her. 'All's fair in love and war, so they say.'

Jancy pummelled her fists against his chest, ignoring the quickening of her pulses. 'You promised you'd leave me alone. Let me go this instant. I don't want to dance with you.'

His eyes saddened. 'It was a promise I could not keep. You're driving me to distraction, do you know that? Every time I catch sight of you I want to drag you back to my cabin and make love.'

'And that's all you want me for,' snapped Jancy.

'Is that what you think?' He sounded hurt.

'It's what I know. You once accused me of seducing you—now it seems the boot's on the other foot. You don't fool me that you've had a change of heart. What we had going for us was

good, we both know that, and you just want
another taste of it. But it's not on, Saxon, and the
sooner you realise that the better.'

As she spoke he pulled her even closer and she
felt the erratic thud of his heart. Why was she
perjuring herself? she wondered. Why was she
denying herself to Saxon when her whole body
craved him? It was an insane situation. If only she
wasn't frightened to trust him again. But having
been on the receiving end of his cruel tongue a
couple of times she had no wish to repeat the
experience. 'I demand that you let me go.'

'When I'm good and ready, my little Maid
Marion.' His eyes had hardened at the condemning
tone of her voice, his mouth become grim. 'No
one's going to miss you, least of all Giles. This is
the third dance he's had with the Christmas tree
fairy. I think we ought to do the honourable thing
and leave them alone.' With that he whisked her
out of the ballroom and on to the open deck.

It was a star-spangled night, the air warm and
balmy, the ship cutting its way through an endless
sea. It was a night for lovers.

Saxon leaned back against the rail and pulled
her to him. He tore off his mask and flung it
overboard where it was carried away in the ship's
wake. More gently he took off Jancy's mask, his
fingers cupping her face as he looked at her. She
found herself drugged by the hypnotic quality of
those blue eyes. She could not tear herself away.

Her heart drummed in her ears as he began a
slow tortuous assault of her senses, first of all
feathering her face with kisses, not leaving one
inch of it untouched—her brows, her eyelids, her
nose, the soft contours of her cheeks; nibbling her
ears, finally claiming her mouth.

Even then his kiss was not eager and hungry as she expected—as she wanted even. His lips brushed hers with the lightness of a butterfly's wing, moving across them, teasing, tantalising, turning her bones to water. He explored their outline with the tip of his tongue, withdrawing when Jancy moaned and arched herself against him, wanting more and all of what this man had to offer.

'Not yet, my sweet maid.'

Why was he doing this? she asked herself a thousand times as his mouth slid down the slender column of her throat, resting on the wildly throbbing pulse at its base. At the same time his hands created pleasures of their own, moving slowly and sensually over her back, down to her waist, finally moulding her hips against the hardness of his thighs.

She was aware of his throbbing passion, even though his movements were carefully tempered. Whatever he was trying to do to her he was certainly succeeding. Jancy felt as though she was going out of her mind, her body was burning up, and she longed for him to hasten his motions. How could he control himself?

The high necked cotton dress she wore prevented him from more intimate exploration of her body, but when his hand cupped her breast she could almost imagine that she was naked. Her breathing grew rapid and alarm bells sounded in her head, but even so she allowed him to carry on touching her. She felt as though she was going to melt in his arms and the next time his mouth claimed hers she parted her lips willingly.

For the moment nothing except her love for Saxon mattered. Her whole body craved him so that she passed through the thin dividing line where sanity ended and sheer primitive desire began.

'Jancy, Jancy, I want you so.' The thick husky tones of his voice revealed his inner torment. He was treading the same knife edge as herself.

'Me too,' she whispered.

'Then let's go to my cabin.'

With his arm about her shoulders Jancy walked trance-like at his side. In the lift they fell into each other's arms again, kissing hungrily, urgently, stopping only when the lift doors opened.

In his room Saxon quickly shed his clothing. His hard muscular body excited her, adding to the destructive emotions which raged within.

With hands that were both eager and gentle he undressed her too. She trembled like a fragile flower beneath a gentle breeze. Saxon's hands were not steady either.

When he had completely disrobed her he stood back. 'You're the most beautiful woman God ever created. I was a fool to let you go. I must have been insane to believe all those lies. Come to me, my Jancy. Come to me willingly.'

Unable to tear her eyes away from his face Jancy stepped into his outstretched arms, drawing in a swift ecstatic breath when she felt his hair-roughened skin against her own silken softness. Was there anything in the world so erotic as the feel of this wonderful male animal? He excited her like no one else ever had.

There was an expression on his face she had never seen before; pain and wonder, humility and desire. She lifted her face, arching herself towards him. 'Kiss me, Saxon, kiss me.'

So desperately did she want him that the blood

pounded in her ears. Her whole body ached with a longing that both frightened and thrilled her. Yet still he held back.

'Tell me you love me, Jancy.' His eyes had deepened to a dramatic midnight blue and were fixed on her face as if he was trying to read her answer before she gave it.

Oh, she did, *she did*! Yet even in this heightened state she was conscious of the fact that it was dangerous to give away her true feelings. He thought they were purely physical and it was best it should remain this way. Once committed there would be no backing out.

His heart pounded against her shoulder and she marvelled again at his willpower. He wanted her as much as she wanted him. Why was he waiting? Why was it necessary for him to know how she felt? Wasn't it sufficient that they needed each other?

And then came a pounding on the door. Jancy jumped and stiffened in his arms.

'Damn!' said Saxon thickly. Reluctantly he let her go and began dragging on his trousers. 'Who is it?' he called, hopping from one foot to the other in his haste.

Jancy too began to scramble into her dress, halting only when she heard the voice on the other side of the door.

'It's Giles. I want to speak to Jancy, I know she's in there.'

Her mouth fell open and she shot Saxon a shocked and worried glance. 'I can't let him see me like this.'

'Why not?' asked Saxon grimly, picking up his shirt.

'What will he think?'

'That he's losing the battle. Perhaps I ought to tell him that it's already lost?'

'You can't,' she whispered, half scared.

'Can't I?' Saxon's brows rose mockingly. 'Wait till he sees you. I won't have to tell him.'

He strode to the door and before Jancy could stop him had swung it wide. Giles looked straight past the doctor, his eyes hardening visibly when he saw her half-dressed state, the flush to her cheeks, the brilliance in her eyes.

'Sorry you let her out of your sight?' asked Saxon cruelly.

'I'm sorry I ever came on this cruise.' Giles was in the grip of a barely controlled anger. 'But at this moment I'm more concerned for my mother than what's going on between you two.'

In an instant Saxon changed. 'What's wrong with her?' he asked briskly.

Jancy wished with all her heart that she could have prevented this confrontation. It was so clear what they had been doing—and Giles loved her. How hurt he must be.

'She's in a highly distressed state of mind,' said Giles. 'She saw you two leave but it was not until the unmasking that she realised it was not me Jancy was with.'

Jancy groaned and closed her eyes, her face distorted with misery and regret.

'So what are you suggesting?' asked Saxon. 'That Jancy goes back with you and all will be forgiven? Why don't you admit that you've lost her? Surely your mother wouldn't wish you to enter into a loveless marriage?'

'I love Jancy.' Giles eyed the other man defiantly.

'But does she love you?' Saxon glanced from

him to Jancy, who had by now finished dressing and stood listening, her horror growing by the minute. 'Though I think you know the answer to that. She'd hardly be here with me if she did.'

'I have no wish to discuss our relationship with you,' said Giles tightly.

'Not even though you know it concerns me equally? I told you the other day Jancy was my girl. I meant it, Giles. By fair means or foul I mean to have her.'

Jancy caught Giles' arm. 'Let's go,' she said chokingly, giving Saxon an imploring glance, willing him not to stop her.

Saxon's smile was cruel. 'My time will come. I'm winning slowly but surely. Make sure you remember that, Giles. Take Jancy now, make your peace with your mother, if that's what you wish, but never forget that I intend being the victor.'

Jancy did not know how Giles restrained himself, aware that it was only for her sake he kept his temper under control. But once outside Saxon's cabin, with the door firmly shut between them, he rounded on her, and she realised that his anger was as much against herself as the doctor.

'How could you behave so stupidly? I've tried to help you even though it hurts me to see you throwing your love away on that selfish bastard, but I expected you to play your part too. Surely you realised someone would see you going off with him?'

Jancy felt a heel. 'At first I thought he was you,' she said miserably. 'He dressed up the same. He tricked me!'

'But you must have found out before you went with him? I've had enough, Jancy. I was prepared to go along with our mock engagement because I wanted my mother's peace of mind—but not to the extent of sitting back and letting you make a fool of me.'

'I'm sorry,' she husked, 'I wish I'd never let you do it. I feel so badly about the way I've treated you. I should never have agreed to an engagement. All it's doing is hurting you. I should have told you right from the beginning that there was no hope.'

'I think I knew,' he said sadly. 'I have only myself to blame. But you could have been more discreet. Now we have to tell my mother. I hope you're feeling strong. I thought she was going to throw a fit when she discovered you'd gone off with Saxon. She asked me how I could have stood there and let it happen.'

'What are we going to say to her?' asked Jancy worriedly.

'Certainly not that I caught you in the act of making love. I apologise if I intruded at the wrong moment.' He sounded particularly bitter.

'We hadn't done anything,' said Jancy. 'In fact I'm glad you came. I'd have felt angry with myself afterwards. It's just that when I'm with him I can't help myself. He drugs my senses so that I act in a way that's entirely alien to me.'

'He doesn't drug you,' said Giles gruffly. 'You love him. That's why you do what you do. You're insane to go on fighting it.'

'But it's no good loving a man you don't trust. I have to fight him, Giles.'

He sighed. 'Then you're on your own. I can't go through with our arrangement.'

'But your mother—we can't upset her.'

He snorted angrily. 'You've already done that.

She wouldn't want me to marry you now. She says you're not the girl she thought you were.'

Jancy swallowed hard. 'I guess I'm not. I don't even seem to know myself these days. Perhaps it's this cruise. I'm sure most people here do and say things they wouldn't normally. A sort of letting your hair down.'

He shrugged, unconvinced.

'I suppose I've lost my job as well?'

His lips twisted wryly. 'I'm afraid so. But you could always go back to the hospital.'

She nodded. 'Especially now that Saxon's no longer there. He was the reason I left. Perhaps I will. Do I really have to face your mother tonight?'

'I'm afraid you do,' he said. 'She won't rest until this thing's been sorted out. She's waiting for us now in her cabin.'

Jancy groaned inwardly. 'I'm sorry it's not you I love, Giles. I hate myself for what I've done to you.'

'Don't,' he said, lips compressed. 'I'm desperately unhappy about the situation, and very hurt that you could not go through with our plan. But above all I want you to be happy, and if that means I have to lose you then that's the way it is.'

Jancy's guilt weighed more heavily upon her and by the time they reached the cabin she felt ready to break down. She had no idea how she was going to face her employer, and when she saw the grim displeasure on Mrs Fairfax's face she felt like backing out and running. Due to her own selfish behaviour she had turned what had promised to be a splendid evening into a disaster.

Meekly she stood in front of the woman who sat side by side with Jacob Honeydew on the settee that was Jancy's bed.

'Have you nothing to say?' demanded Mrs

Fairfax imperiously. 'Have you no heart, girl? Don't you realise what you have done to my son?'

'I think, Mother,' said Giles, 'that the time has come for me to tell you that our plans for marriage fell through after the day Jancy spent on Martinique with Saxon. We kept up the act for your sake. We wanted you to enjoy your trip.'

'But you love Jancy!' said his mother incredulously.

'Yes, but Jancy doesn't love me.'

'You mean you lied?' Her voice rose hysterically.

Jancy did not like the colour of Mrs Fairfax's face. 'Do calm down. Giles and I knew exactly what we were doing.'

'Are you trying to tell me that you love Saxon Marriot?' asked the woman harshly. 'And that it is he you intend marrying?'

Jancy shook her head. 'I'm not going to marry Saxon—or Giles, I'm afraid.'

'You mean you're playing around with both of them?' Mrs Fairfax's eyes bulged.

The admiral laid a hand on her arm. 'Fiona, dear, don't get yourself worked up. Let these young people sort out their own affairs. There's nothing you can do.'

'Nothing I can do? It's my son I'm concerned about. I can't let him make a mess of his life.'

'I'm not making a mess of it, Mother,' said Giles. 'I knew how Jancy felt towards me. I won't be the first person in the world to have loved a woman who does not love him in return.'

'She's a hussy,' said Mrs Fairfax crisply. 'She's pulled the wool over both our eyes. Consider yourself sacked, Jancy. Your services are no longer required.'

Jancy hung her head. There was no point in arguing. The wisest course was to give in quietly. Causing Mrs Fairfax further distress could bring on a heart attack, and that she must avoid at all costs.

'I only wish you could be moved to some other cabin,' continued the older woman. 'It's a pity the ship's full.'

It took all Jancy's self-control to refrain from answering back, telling herself she must remember this woman's condition. 'I'll keep out of your way as much as possible,' she said, turning towards the door.

She followed Giles into his cabin across the corridor and they sat down on the edge of his bunk. 'I've made a mess of everything, haven't I?' she said. 'I've even made you hate me. I shall be glad when this cruise is over.'

He heaved a sigh. 'I don't hate you, Jancy, I'm disappointed. I feel let down. I did think you'd make an effort for the few days that remained. Saxon told me he'd win you back, but I didn't believe him. I didn't want to believe him. Now it looks as though he was right.'

Jancy shook her head. 'Every time I've been with Saxon it's because he forced me into it. I've never gone of my own free will. I could never be happy with a man who shoves me around, who inflicts his will upon my own. When I make up my mind to marry it will be my own decision, not someone else's.'

'I certainly hope it will be mutual,' said Giles.

'That too,' agreed Jancy, 'but I don't want anyone telling me what's right, what I should do and what I shouldn't do. He's a pig and I hate him.'

Giles shook his head disbelievingly, but said nothing. He poured her a glass of sherry and they sat drinking quietly, remaining there long after they heard the admiral leave.

It was with reluctance that Jancy finally made her way back to the cabin she shared with Mrs Fairfax, desperately hoping to find her in bed and asleep.

Mrs Fairfax was indeed in bed but she was not asleep, and was clearly awaiting Jancy's return, calling out the moment the door opened. 'Jancy, come here. I want to speak to you.'

Jancy's stomach turned but she obeyed.

'Why weren't you straight with me from the beginning, girl? You told me you knew Saxon, but not the extent of your relationship, that he was the one you were running away from. Why was that? If I'd known I would never have let you go off with him. I feel it is my fault all this has happened.'

'I didn't think it was anyone's business but my own and Saxon's,' said Jancy softly. 'It was such a shock seeing him here I didn't want to talk about him. I didn't mean to upset you, Mrs Fairfax.'

'It's only because I don't think you've been fair on my son that I'm upset. I find it difficult to believe that you got engaged to Giles knowing you did not love him.'

'I thought it would work,' said Jancy miserably. 'When Giles found out how I felt he agreed to carry on with the engagement to protect me from Saxon. I feel awful about it. Your son's such a nice person.'

Mrs Fairfax snorted. 'He didn't make a very good job of protecting you—or perhaps you didn't want to be protected?'

'I did, I did,' cried Jancy. 'Saxon tricked me tonight, dressing up as Robin Hood. He must have somehow discovered what Giles was going to wear.'

'It appears to me,' said Mrs Fairfax, 'that you love this Saxon Marriot, otherwise you'd give him his marching orders.'

'I've tried,' said Jancy tiredly. 'Believe me, I've tried. He just doesn't take no for an answer.'

'Then you can't have been very convincing. Do you love him?'

The bluntness of her question surprised Jancy. 'I suppose I do.'

'Then why are you messing him around? You must surely realise that it's not only your own life you're upsetting, but mine and Giles', and Saxon's too.'

Jancy shook her head again. 'Saxon once let me down very badly. I don't feel I can trust him again.'

'In that case why have anything to do with him?'

'Because he's a forceful personality. He's convinced that I don't know my own mind. He's very determined to make me marry him.'

Mrs Fairfax shook her head impatiently. 'If you want nothing more to do with him then tell him point blank. Don't be satisfied until he accepts your answer. Would you like me to do it for you?'

'Of course not,' said Jancy quickly. 'I can handle my own affairs.'

'It looks like it,' snorted Mrs Fairfax. 'If there's to be any peace for the remainder of this cruise go and sort yourself out—now.'

'But it's after midnight,' protested Jancy. 'I can't go to his cabin at this hour.'

'Then send for him,' said the woman imperiously.

'I'd rather be alone.' Jancy felt appalled at the thought of discussing her private affairs in front of Mrs Fairfax.

'Then you must do it first thing in the morning—and let's hope we all get some sleep.'

But Jancy did not sleep. She tossed and turned, trying to decide what to say to Saxon, how to convince him. She doubted whether he would accept her word. She had tried so many times in the past. But somehow she had to do it. As Mrs Fairfax said, it was the only way any of them were going to get any peace.

Her whole future hinged on this meeting. If she failed to make Saxon believe it was all over she would end up marrying him—and what sort of life would she create for herself then?

It was the longest night of Jancy's life and when morning arrived she felt drained. There were dark shadows beneath her eyes and even a shower did not refresh her.

Mrs Fairfax was sleeping peacefully as she crept out and went up on deck, putting off the evil moment for as long as possible. The lacy whiteness of the bow wave failed to entrance her. She looked at it with dulled eyes, conscious only of the task that was looming closer.

Then she saw Giles looking over the rail. It was unusual for him to be doing nothing at this hour. He had on a pair of white slacks and a blue shirt so had certainly not been jogging. He was lost in a world of his own, unaware of Jancy's presence.

She stood for a moment wondering whether to speak to him. It was her fault he was in this mood. She felt awful about the whole thing. Why couldn't she love someone as nice as Giles? Why did it have to be Saxon, the one man guaranteed to hurt her?

Suddenly Giles turned and she was shocked by the despair on his face. He looked like a man who had lost everything. His eyes were dull, his mouth downturned, and all of his vital energy had disappeared.

When he saw Jancy he made a brave effort to pull himself together, smiling weakly. 'Hello, Jancy. I didn't know you were there.'

'I can see that,' she said sadly. 'Giles, I really do apologise for the way I treated you. It was most unfair.'

'Don't be sorry,' he said. 'I brought it on myself. I thought there was hope—until I saw you together last night. That's when I realised there would never be a place for me in your heart.'

'I'll always remember you,' she said.

'And me you,' came the bitter response. 'Please go away now, Jancy. It would be best if we avoid each other as much as possible for the rest of this voyage. I can't——' He broke off abruptly and swung away, walking crisply along the deck.

Jancy watched him sadly until he turned a corner. If she had been feeling rotten before, she felt ten times worse now. Giles was a broken man—and all because of her. It must have been agony for him. She was tempted to go after him, beg his forgiveness, but knew this would make things worse. Giles was right—it was best they keep out of each other's way.

Finally Jancy plucked up the courage to go and see Saxon, firming her chin as she made her way below, praying she would find the right words.

There was no answer when she tapped on his cabin door. She guessed he was in the hospital but was reluctant to face him in front of his nurses. Then her decision was made for her. As she stood in the corridor dithering one of the nurses came out. 'The doctor's in here if you're after him,' she called, and as if to add conviction to her words he too appeared in the doorway.

'Come in, Jancy,' he said, as his nurse walked away. She glanced anxiously about her.

'It's all right, we're quite alone. What brings you down here so early?'

He looked fresh and relaxed, his eyes bright, hair neatly combed, his usual crisp white shirt outlining the lithe maleness of his body. It was evident he had lost no sleep.

'I can't go on with this cat and mouse game any longer.' She paused and swallowed painfully, still assailed by last minute doubts, still finding him as physically exciting as ever.

His smile was infinitely gentle as he put his hands on her shoulders. 'I'm glad you've come to your senses.'

She shook her head desperately and backed away. 'It's not what you think, Saxon.'

His eyes expressed disbelief. 'You mean you've decided to marry Giles after all?'

'No,' she whispered, feeling her heart crash painfully against her rib-cage. 'I'm not going to marry Giles, but I'm not going to marry you either.'

Their eyes met and locked for an endless minute, then he grasped her again, shaking her roughly. 'You don't know what you're saying.'

Pain shot through her as she struggled to escape, but his grip merely tightened. 'I know I've lost my job over you,' she snapped. 'You've made me the unhappiest woman in the world.'

His eyes darkened. 'I didn't mean to do that, Jancy.'

'You haven't meant to do a lot of things,' she spat.

'And I'm sorry you've lost your job. Naturally, you're upset over it but if you marry me you won't need to work.'

Jancy shook her head desperately. 'When are you going to realise that I shall never marry you?' Her heart pounded and her head throbbed, and she renewed her struggles to escape.

With a groan he slid his hands behind her back and crushed her against him. 'Jancy, my love, you're confused. You don't know what you're saying.'

'I know all right,' she cried. 'Let me go! This is insanity.' She could feel the throb of his heart against her, smell the clean maleness of him. And he knew that this was the one sure-fire way of getting through to her!

Like a wildcat she clawed. 'You swine, Saxon Marriot. Let me go! Let me go this instant!'

His smile was grim. 'Not until you promise to come to your senses.'

'It's you who's insane,' she cried. 'You can't impose your will on me, I won't let you. I have a right to make up my own mind.'

'Unfortunately, you do not always make the right decision,' he said.

'Neither do you,' she declared. 'You decided once that I was not a nice sort of girl.'

'But I came to my senses. And you will too if you'll only allow yourself to overcome your mistrust.'

His mouth was dangerously close, his blue eyes ablaze with a fierce light that both thrilled and scared her. She renewed her struggles, putting her hands on his shoulders and pushing with all her might, but to no avail. She might as well have saved her strength.

He fought her with the only weapon he knew would guarantee success. There was no way that she could resist his kisses. They melted her bones, turned her blood to water, and spun her senses until she was no longer in control of her feelings.

When finally he set her mouth free Jancy's lungs were bursting and she drank in great gulps of air, but still his arms imprisoned her. He put his ear to her heart. 'You're like a captured bird,' he said softly, 'but have no fear, my little one, I'm not going to harm you.'

'You couldn't hurt me any more,' she said huskily.

Abruptly he straightened. 'Am I going to be punished for the rest of my life for what was after all a very simple misunderstanding?'

'Simple?' she queried disbelievingly. 'It was sufficient to turn you against me.'

'No man likes to feel he's been tricked.'

'And no woman likes to feel her integrity threatened.'

'*Touché*,' he said. 'But as we both now know it was a mistake surely there's no reason why we can't get back together?'

Jancy felt his hands burning her and knew that the longer she remained in his arms the weaker her resolve would become. But she also knew that struggling would get her nowhere. She stood limp, indeed wondered whether she would collapse if he let her go. 'There's one very big reason,' she said.

'And that is?'

'There's no proof that your nasty suspicious mind won't read something into an innocent situation again. It's the sort of man you are, Saxon. I can't take that chance.'

He shook his head. 'You're making an issue out of nothing.'

'I don't think it's nothing,' she said. 'You may as well give up. You're wasting your time.'

With a suddenness that was surprising he let her go, moving to the other side of the room. Then he turned and looked at her. 'Answer me one question, Jancy—truthfully. If the answer is not what I expect then I'll let you go, and I give my word that I'll not pester you again.'

Jancy felt her heart stop. She thought she knew what his question was going to be. For several long seconds it was as though time stood still, then he said, 'Do you love me, Jancy? The truth, mind. Your whole future, and mine, depends on your answer.'

It took Jancy a long time to reach her decision. She was essentially an honest girl and it went against the grain to lie. But if she wanted peace of mind in the future then she had to lie now—and do it convincingly. She swung away. 'I did love you, Saxon,' she said quietly, 'but not any longer.'

'Look at me and say it.' His words shot across the room like bullets from a gun.

Very slowly she turned, drawing in a quick violent breath when she saw the tense pallor of his face. She wanted to run to him, put her arms around him, and say, no, she hadn't meant it. But that was not the answer.

Somehow she made herself look into his eyes, fixed him with an unblinking stare. Deep down inside she uttered a little prayer for forgiveness. 'I don't love you, Saxon.' The words were shaky but her eyes did not waver.

'Say it again.' His voice was hoarse.

'God, what have I got to do, put my hand on a Bible?' cried Jancy. 'Isn't my word enough? Don't you believe me?'

He nodded, his head seeming too heavy for his shoulders. 'Yes, I believe you. That's one thing I do know about you, Jancy, that you wouldn't lie. Not over something as serious as this. I know you lied about your engagement to Giles, but that was self-protection.'

His shoulders sagged and he looked suddenly old, his feet dragging as he crossed the room towards her. Very slowly and very tenderly he pressed a kiss to her brow. 'Goodbye, Jancy. Goodbye.'

She felt the sting of tears behind her eyes and in that moment wanted to throw herself into his arms and declare her love. But she made herself recall the callous way he had treated her, the harsh accusations he had flung at her, the way he had cast her out of his life; and firming her shoulders she turned and walked out of the room.

CHAPTER EIGHT

WITH tears streaming down her face Jancy walked slowly along the corridor away from the hospital. She had sealed her fate. Whether it was a right or wrong decision only time would tell.

She walked blindly, not heeding where she went, unaware of the curious glances directed her way. She found herself in the library, deserted at this hour, and sat down in a hidden corner. She cried until there were no tears left, silent sobs which caused a pain in her chest and an ache in her heart.

All she could do now was wait for the end of the voyage and make a new start. She would not even go back to the General. She would go away, somewhere different altogether, somewhere where there was no chance of her bumping into Saxon Marriot.

Eventually she returned to her cabin, informing Mrs Fairfax that she had done as she suggested. 'It's all over between us now. He's finally accepted that I want nothing more to do with him.'

Mrs Fairfax sniffed indelicately. 'A pity you didn't show such strength of mind in the first place. You've completely ruined the holiday—for all of us.'

'I know, and I'm sorry,' whispered Jancy, relieved when the woman swept out of the room. She changed into a comfortable cotton sundress, gathered up her sunglasses and a book, and found herself a secluded corner on one of the decks. But although the book lay open in her hands and her eyes were turned towards it she read none of the printed pages, conscious only of a heavy melancholy.

'How would you like to join me in a game of tennis?' Giles' voice broke into her depression.

Jancy raised her eyes, looking at him blankly. 'I don't think I have the energy.' Poor Giles, he too looked as though the bottom had dropped out of his world.

'Or the inclination?' he asked gently.

She shook her head.

'Sitting here brooding won't help.'

'It's all I can do,' she answered. 'I've finished with Saxon completely.'

'Yes, I know,' came his surprising answer. 'I bumped into him a short time ago. He told me it was all over between you. In fact he shook my hand and wished me all the best.'

Jancy's fine brows shot up.

'He said that he'd made a mistake in assuming he could win you back.'

'I think I've made a mistake, too,' said Jancy sadly.

'You've done what you thought best.' Giles squatted down beside her and took her hands. 'You'll get over him—in time. Just as I'll get over you. If you don't want to play tennis how about a drink to commiserate our misfortunes in falling in love with the wrong person?'

Jancy smiled wanly and nodded. They went into the Columbine Bar which, with its cerise banquettes and carpet, its timeless elegance, suited her mood perfectly. This room was not used so much during the day, the bigger Flamingo Bar being mostly favoured, and it was good to get away from the crowds.

Giles ordered her a gin and tonic and she drank it quickly, asking for another. His brows rose but he gave her order, frowning when she drank that one too the moment it arrived. 'Take care, Jancy, this isn't the answer.'

The effects of the gin on her empty stomach made her feel reckless. 'Who do you think you're talking to? You're not a doctor.' Her head felt distinctly light and when she attempted to stand the room began to swim. She sat down again quickly.

Giles said, 'Have you eaten today?'

Her eyes widened. What a stupid question! Of course she had eaten, it was past lunchtime. But when she gave the matter more thought she realised that she'd had nothing at all. 'What's it matter to you?' she asked, wondering whether that slurred voice really belonged to her. Two drinks surely couldn't have such an effect?

But they must have done for when she again tried to stand she stumbled and would have fallen had Giles not caught her. 'Come on,' he said. 'I'll take you to your cabin and arrange some sandwiches.'

'I'm not hungry,' insisted Jancy.

But Giles was obdurate. 'You'll eat even if I have to force it down you. You're being stupid. God knows what you're trying to achieve.' With his arm still about her shoulders they made their way below.

It was Jancy's bad luck that they bumped into Saxon Marriot. He did not miss Giles' arm about her, Jancy's head on his shoulder. His mouth was a thin hard line as he passed them by without a word. They could have been a couple of strangers. She found it difficult to believe that he had cut her out of his life so completely.

The sandwiches were tastefully arranged, garnished with tomatoes and cress, but Jancy only managed two of the tiny triangles of freshly baked bread.

'I'd never have bought you those gins if I'd known,' said Giles. 'There's no point in starving yourself. You've still got to live your life no matter what sort of a mess it's in.'

'I wish I was as strong as you,' she said. 'You must be feeling equally as broken-hearted.'

He smiled wryly. 'Think how boring it would be if we had everything we wanted.'

'That's one way of looking at it,' she replied. 'And you're right, Giles, I'm not doing myself any good by being miserable.'

'That's a good girl. I think you ought to try and get some sleep now. You look all in.'

He went out and closed the door softly. Jancy put her head down and knew no more until she heard Mrs Fairfax getting ready for dinner.

Jancy had no intention of going into the restaurant that evening. She could not face Saxon Marriot again. So she pretended to be still asleep when she heard the woman leave.

But she had not counted on Giles' determination. He came in to her minutes only after his mother had gone. 'Come along, Jancy,' he said. 'Get yourself ready. You're not going without another meal.'

She looked at him, her eyes wide. 'I can't face Saxon.'

'He won't be there,' he advised. 'There's an emergency. Someone's broken a leg. He'll be busy for quite a while.'

'But I'm not really hungry.' She looked at him appealingly.

'You're going! I'll give you five minutes to get ready.' He left before she could argue further and Jancy knew that what he said made sense.

She showered and slipped on one of the fine evening dresses Mrs Fairfax had bought her, feeling uneasy now that she was no longer in the woman's employ.

She ate more than she expected but was glad when the meal was over. Mrs Fairfax acknowledged her presence, but that was all, and although no one else at the table seemed to sense the atmosphere Jancy felt distinctly uncomfortable.

The following day the weather changed dramatically and yet another of those rare storms blew up as they passed the coast of Cuba.

But it was not this that caused the excitement. The captain's voice came over the loudspeaker informing that there had been an explosion on a Cuban fishing vessel and they were going to turn round and go to its aid.

Naturally everyone rushed up on deck, some still in pyjamas and nightdresses with jackets pulled hurriedly over them, heedless of the rain mercilessly lashing the decks.

Jancy pulled on a pair of jeans and a sweater, with a waterproof anorak over the top. She had packed it on the spur of the moment, not really thinking she might need it, but having heard reports of the uncertainty of the Bermudan weather it had seemed the right thing to do. Now she was glad.

The seas were heaving and as the ship cut an arc Jancy clung to the rail for dear life. It was stupid standing there and getting drenched, but everyone was doing it. This was a moment of excitement, something to tell their friends about when they got home.

All eyes eagerly scanned the raging seas, looking
for the tiny vessel that was in trouble. A shout
went up when they saw her and the lifeboat was
swung into position ready to be lowered the
moment they were close enough.

It had not occurred to Jancy that Saxon might
be involved but when she saw him she was not
surprised. If there was someone hurt then a doctor
would be needed.

Smoke rose from the fishing boat but no one was
in sight. Jancy watched with bated breath as the
lifeboat was lowered into the heaving sea. The liner
had gone as near as she dare. It was now up to them.

There were murmurs all around as it rode the
waves, drawing slowly nearer to the unfortunate
fishing vessel. How, she wondered, were they
going to manage when the waves tossed each boat
like flotsam? When one was up the other was
down. There looked no chance that the two of
them would ever remain still enough for the men
to board her.

The crew hailed the boat and a lone fisherman
appeared. A line was cast across, several attempts
having to be made before it finally reached its
target and was secured.

Then to Jancy's horror Saxon began to haul
himself inch by inch along the rope, hands and
ankles locked around it. There were times when his
whole body was immersed in the raging seas, at
others he was high and dry, the line stretched so
taut Jancy felt sure it would snap.

Why Saxon? she asked herself in anguish, one
hand clasped over her mouth, the other gripping
the rail of the rolling ship. Why Saxon? Why not
one of the others? He was not trained for such
things. His whole life was in danger.

She was afraid to bat an eyelid, reluctant to take her eyes off him for one second. And then her worst fears were realised. A wave more angry and more vicious than any other sucked at his battling body, plucking with fingers of steel, not relenting until with a shout Saxon fell into the boiling foam beneath.

Jancy's scream followed, together with cries from all those watching. He was tossed like a cork, his bright orange lifejacket all that could be seen. With a fortitude that amazed her he began to swim towards the fishing boat, pitting his strength against the might of the ocean.

His progress was slow, at times he was swept back and had to begin all over again, but bravely he kept going.

Meantime the crew on the lifeboat, by means of the rope, were drawing the fishing vessel as near as they dare. Too close and they would end up as matchwood, tossed for ever on the storm-ridden seas. But every inch was one less for Saxon to swim and at length he was close enough to be hauled on board by the waiting fisherman.

Even that was a feat of endurance, every time their fingers touched the greedy sea dragged Saxon away, but eventually he made it.

In that moment Jancy knew she could not live without him, she could not let him go. She had almost lost him then, but miraculously he had been saved. She must tell him she loved him. He would take some convincing, but it had to be done. She loved him desperately, beyond all measure. Life without Saxon was unthinkable.

It was strange how it had taken those long heart-stopping minutes to make her realise that she loved him more dearly than anything or anyone in the whole world. What did it matter that he had a quick temper, that he might sometimes accuse her of something she hadn't done? She could live with that. He loved her too, she was sure of it now. Why else had he wanted to start anew? Why else would he have admitted he was in the wrong?

He was not the type of man to apologise. He must have wanted her very much, had indeed been trying to find her. But she, wrapped up in her own stupid selfishness, had given no thought to his feelings.

It seemed like hours before the injured fishermen were winched one by one on board the *Ocean Queen*. The surgeon followed shortly afterwards and Jancy did not wait for the rest of the crew to come aboard. Her concern was for Saxon.

She followed below to the hospital, but was stopped outside by one of the nurses. 'There are some pretty bad burns. We shall all be kept busy for the next few hours. I should appreciate it if you'd keep out of the way.'

Jancy wondered whether the girl was aware of the rift between her and Saxon, whether she had been instructed to keep her away. She turned tiredly and went to her cabin.

Mrs Fairfax was horrified when she saw Jancy's bedraggled appearance. She had missed the announcement and was aware only that they were in the grip of a storm. 'You silly child, what on earth made you go up on deck?'

'There was an accident, didn't you know?' said Jancy. 'An explosion on a fishing boat. We went to its rescue.'

'Was anyone hurt?' Mrs Fairfax's eyes widened with surprise.

Jancy nodded. 'They're in the hospital now. Saxon went with the lifeboat.' She gulped, and tears that she had fought back for so long suddenly surfaced. 'He almost lost his life. For one awful moment I thought he was going to drown.' Her voice faded as emotion took over. 'Oh, Mrs Fairfax, I do love him. I think I'd have died if anything had happened.'

The woman took her into her arms. 'There, there,' she said, 'it's all over. I'm sure you worried for nothing.'

She didn't know the half, thought Jancy, swallowing, dabbing ineffectively at her tears. 'I've been such a fool. I've upset Giles, and you, and everyone, just because I was trying to get my own back on Saxon.'

'It often takes something like this to bring us to our senses,' said Mrs Fairfax sagely. 'I said some hasty things to you myself. I suppose I was trying to protect Giles, though Lord knows he's old enough to take care of himself. I shall never forget what you did, but Giles is too sensible to let it ruin the rest of his life. And I'm happy with Jacob, so I hope, Jancy, that you too will find happiness.'

'I hope so,' said Jancy fervently. 'I just hope I haven't left it too late.'

For the rest of the day Jancy did nothing but wander aimlessly about the ship. News filtered through that there were no fatalities and that the men were fairly comfortable despite the severity of their burns. Jancy desperately wanted to see Saxon, she wanted to talk to him, but knew she dare not venture anywhere near the hospital. He did not show up in the restaurant at any of the meal times and Jancy grew more and more depressed.

She suspected he was avoiding her deliberately. He had accepted her decision and that was it. He would not know that she had changed her mind. She simply must see him.

There was one certain way of getting him to her cabin, and that was to say that Mrs Fairfax was ill. But she was reluctant to do this. He would be angry when he discovered she had summoned him under false pretences, and an angry Saxon she did not want to deal with. She needed him in a good humour.

On the other hand they would soon be back in Miami. She wanted everything sorted out by then, not relishing the idea of chasing after him in his new clinic, or his flat. Besides, the atmosphere on board was conducive to romance, there was a much greater possibility that she could persuade him she was speaking the truth.

When the last day came and the *Ocean Queen* approached the Florida coast and Jancy had still not seen Saxon she knew there was nothing for it but to ask him to come to the cabin. She waited until Mrs Fairfax was out somewhere with Jacob and then rang the hospital. To her dismay Saxon himself answered, but she spoke resolutely. 'You're needed here at once.' There was an urgency in her tone to which she knew he would respond.

Within half a minute he was at the door and Jancy led him apprehensively inside. He hardly glanced at her, marching straight through to Mrs Fairfax's bedroom, pulling up short when he saw it empty. He swung round. 'Is this some sort of joke?'

His face was as hard as she had ever seen it, looking almost as though it had been hewn out of granite. Jancy swallowed with difficulty and made herself look at him. 'It's very serious.'

'But Mrs Fairfax is not ill, nor are you by the look of it.'

'I'm desperately unhappy,' she said, deciding to go straight into it. 'I made the biggest mistake of my life telling you I didn't want to marry you.'

His eyes narrowed and Jancy felt herself pinned by his gaze. 'Are you saying that you got me here just to tell me that?'

Jancy nodded. 'I've been looking for you, ever since the accident, but you seem to have been avoiding me.'

'You're damn right I have,' he snapped. 'I'd lived for so long with the thought that we might get back together, and God knows I did my damnedest to make it come true, but you made your point very clear and now I don't wish to see you again.'

Jancy moved tentatively towards him, her arms outstretched. 'You can't mean that, Saxon. Don't you understand? I love you, I want to marry you.'

The cold blueness of his eyes cut through her. 'I don't much care for women who can't make up their mind. What's wrong, doesn't Giles want you either? Are you afraid of being left on the shelf?'

'You know very well that I never intended marrying Giles,' she said.

'Neither did you want to marry me. Why the sudden change?'

'It was when you tried to board that fishing vessel,' she admitted faintly, knowing that nothing but the truth would help her now. 'It brought me to my senses. I realised that if anything happened to you life wouldn't be worth living.'

'Maybe you should have thought of that when

you gave me my marching orders,' he rasped, the stony hardness of his eyes unchanged. 'I'm sorry, Jancy, but that's the way it is. It's all over. You had your chance, I'm not prepared to give you another.' With that he swung away and moved swiftly towards the door.

Jancy could not believe that he was as unmoved as he made out. 'Doesn't it mean anything—that I love you?' she cried, racing across the room and standing with her back to the door, blocking his exit.

His face was expressionless as he looked at her. 'Nothing at all.'

Jancy's stomach knotted, a chill stole over her. She could not believe this. 'But Saxon, you were so insistent that you wanted to marry me. You even had a fight with Giles. I don't believe that you no longer care.'

'Oh, I care all right,' he snarled, 'but who's to say you won't have another change of heart?'

'I won't,' she protested. 'Really, Saxon, you must believe me. You changed your mind, why can't I? I don't want to go on living if I can't marry you.'

'Then do us both a favour and throw yourself overboard,' he said, pushing her roughly to one side. 'You felt nothing but sympathy for me, when you thought I was in danger. I can do without that. I'm going now, Jancy, and, please, don't ever try to see me again.'

He was through the door before she could stop him. Unable to accept that he had walked so coldly out of her life Jancy felt as though she had been turned into a block of stone. Only her mind was alive, her brain in a whirl of confused emotions.

Was this the end then, of her affair with Saxon

Marriot? It looked very much like it. He had made it perfectly clear he wanted nothing more to do with her. She had had her chance and lost it, he was not going to give her another one. It was ironical, considering the way he had run after her.

But there was nothing else she could do. She had swallowed her pride and there was only so far a girl could go. She would certainly not go after him again. There would be no point in it anyway. Although she had changed her mind, Saxon Marriot never would.

It was with a sense of despair that Jancy finally stepped ashore at Port of Miami. She had seen nothing more of Saxon, not that she had expected to. After the flight back to Heathrow she was going with Mrs Fairfax to her house until she had sorted herself out. Giles' attitude towards her was cool, but not unfriendly, for which she was grateful. She had given him a raw deal and it would have served her right had he cast her out of his life altogether, like Saxon.

Jancy did not remain at the Fairfax household for more than a couple of days, recovering from jet lag, packing her possessions and moving in with her sister, Kate. Kate was alarmed to hear that Jancy had met Saxon Marriot again and even more disturbed to hear what had happened.

'I felt guilty when he let you down, because it was at my party you met him.'

Jancy shook her head. 'It had nothing to do with you, Kate, as you well know. We could have met at any time. After all, we did work at the same place. It was simply coincidence.'

'Nevertheless,' said Kate, 'I still feel responsible. But actually I think you're well rid of him. Maybe you do love him, but would marriage work? You could be buying yourself a whole load of trouble. You'd never know when he'd fly off the handle again. He's a very volatile man. If I were you I'd count your blessings.'

It was all very well Kate saying that, thought Jancy despondently. It was what she had thought herself at one time. But Kate didn't love him.

She spent her days moping about the house with no inclination to look for another job. It was her sister who, after a week of Jancy's sombre moods, told her to pull herself together.

'I know I should,' said Jancy, 'but it's hard. I'm going to move away from London altogether, then I needn't worry about bumping into him.'

'Phil has a friend who runs a nursing home in Brighton,' said Kate. 'Shall I ask him to put in a word for you?'

Brighton? That sounded far enough away to be safe, yet not too far to visit her sister. 'Mmm, I think I'd like that.'

So Philip got in touch with his friend and eventually told Jancy that if she cared to go and see Mrs Garrett there was every chance of a job.

Within a week Jancy was settled in the nursing home. The work was not taxing and there were times when Jancy thought of nothing but Saxon Marriot. As the weeks turned into months, however, he was in her mind less frequently. She would never get over him completely, she knew that. There would always be a special place for him in her heart, but the pain was lessening.

At the beginning of December Mrs Garratt announced that she was giving a pre-Christmas party. She knew a lot of people in the medical profession and it looked like being a splash affair.

Jancy was thoroughly looking forward to the

occasion. It had been a long time since she'd enjoyed herself socially, not since the cruise, in fact. Work had seemed the solution to her problem. Now she intended letting down her hair. She had been a recluse too long.

Some of the guests arrived early and Jancy was still fixing her hair when there came a tap on her door. She was surprised to see Mrs Garrett herself. 'There's someone asking after you. A Mr Marriot. I thought I'd let you know.'

'Saxon?' Jancy's face paled. 'What's he doing here?'

'He heard about the party through a mutual friend,' said Mrs Garrett. 'It appears he's come specifically to see you.'

'I can't think why,' said Jancy stiffly. 'And I don't want to see him. We weren't the best of friends when we parted. I should hate to cause a disturbance.'

'In that case,' said her employer, 'why don't you talk to him here? He indicated that what he had to say was very important.'

Jancy could not imagine what it was. She sighed deeply. 'I suppose I'll have to see him.'

Mrs Garrett beamed. 'He was someone special?'

Jancy nodded reluctantly. The woman was as perceptive as Mrs Fairfax, or was it simply that she was no good at hiding her feelings?

'In that case,' said Mrs Garrett, 'I'll see you're not disturbed. He's a fine man, well liked in the medical profession. You couldn't do better.'

Jancy's heart pounded as she waited. She paced the room, checking her reflection in the mirror a dozen times, aware that she looked pale and tense. She dared not even think of the possibility that Saxon had had a change of heart. There must be some other reason he was here.

It seemed an age before he finally came. He looked exactly as she remembered, resplendent in a black dinner suit, his white shirt emphasising the tan he still sported. Jancy felt her emotions well up inside, she glowed with a sudden heat, blood pounded in her head.

'How did you know I was working here?' she asked faintly.

'Your sister,' he announced matter-of-factly.

'Kate? She wouldn't tell you—not unless you gave her some really good excuse for wanting to see me. She hates your guts.'

'Oh, I did,' he assured, 'and this party provided me with the ideal opportunity.' He made no attempt to come into the room, standing with his back to the door, one hand pushed into his trouser pocket. His open jacket revealed the embroidered whiteness of his shirt, the muscular chest beneath.

'So why have you come?' she husked. 'I don't think I can stand any more pain.'

He looked humble all of a sudden. 'I don't want to hurt you, Jancy. I've come to beg your forgiveness. I've come to ask if you will marry me.'

Jancy did not believe in miracles, but this was surely one. 'Why?' she asked quietly.

'Because—I've realised I can't live without you.' He swallowed with difficulty and Jancy resisted the impulse to throw herself into his arms. She stood silently looking at him, her green eyes saucer-wide.

'Aren't you going to say anything?' he asked. 'I thought you'd be delirious.'

'What's made you change your mind?' she demanded bluntly.

'I was stupid.' His voice was rough, full of emotion. 'Too damn proud by half. I knew you

loved me and yet you continually denied yourself
to me. I wanted to kiss you, Jancy. I wanted to get
my hands round your slender neck and squeeze
every little bit of life out of you. Oh, God, Jancy,
why did you do it?' In a couple of strides he was
across the room and had her crushed against his
chest. His heart beat an urgent tattoo, his
breathing as ragged as her own.

'I was afraid to trust you,' she whispered.

'With every right,' he said thickly. 'I was a
bastard. I don't deserve your love. But I want you,
Jancy. I want you to share the rest of your life
with me. Oh God, I love you so much.'

Jancy felt a wave of relief at his words. At last
he had admitted it. 'And I love you,' she said,
lifting her face, unaware that it was shiny with
tears. 'I love you, Saxon, with all my heart.'

He groaned and kissed her with an animal
hunger, holding her so tightly she feared he would
squeeze all the breath out of her body. 'Oh, Jancy,
Jancy,' he murmured thickly. 'Don't ever go out of
my life again.'

'I won't,' she whispered between his kisses. 'The
only way you'll get rid of me now, Saxon, is by
killing me. I've prayed for this day, I've hoped for
it, but I never believed it would happen. Oh,
Saxon, I do love you.'

There was silence as they clung passionately,
their kisses relieving their pent-up emotion of the
last few months. 'God, I needed that,' he said
when he finally put her from him. 'Have you a
drink, Jancy? I sure could do with one.'

'Not here,' she said, 'it's not allowed.'

'Then I'll do without. I certainly don't intend
going downstairs. I'm not sharing you with all
those people, not now, not ever.'

'I can't believe it,' said Jancy, afraid to take her eyes off his beloved face. 'Tell me I'm not dreaming.'

'Touch me,' he said, 'feel me. I'm very much alive. I'm a part of you now, Jancy. We're going to have a wonderful future together.'

'I hope,' she said softly, 'that I can make you as happy as your first wife did.' It was risky, she knew, mentioning this woman, but they could not avoid the subject for ever.

A brief flash of pain crossed his face. 'We were very happy, I freely admit that. She was a remarkable person, a very selfless person. She had a crippling accident, you know, and despite all my medical knowledge I could not help her. She spent the last few years of her life in a wheelchair.'

Jancy gasped, but he went on, 'She knew she was going to die and made me promise I would never worship her memory. "I want you to be happy, Saxon," she said. "I want you to marry again." I never thought I would. I lived in a void after her death. I didn't want anyone else.'

He paused but Jancy was afraid to speak, desperately afraid she might say the wrong thing. She could not afford to turn him away from her again.

'The night I saw you at Phil's party her words came back. I realised what she had been trying to tell me. Life did go on. There were other people equally capable of giving me love, of accepting my love. I hated the way you were dressed but I thought I saw a special woman beneath.'

Jancy felt an enormous lump in her throat, tears flooding afresh. She had known none of this, no one had. They would never have talked about his lack of interest in women had they been aware of the tragic circumstances of his wife's death.

'I was so hurt, Jancy, when I discovered you weren't the perfect angel I was looking for. I should have known differently. I shouldn't have listened to idle gossip. Jancy, my love, will you ever forgive me for the way I treated you?'

'I already have,' she said. 'It took some doing, I must admit. I wanted to get back at you when we met up again, even though I still loved you. That was the ridiculous part about it. I was crazy about you, Saxon. I wish I'd followed my heart instead of dragging Giles and his mother into it. I really hurt them.'

'I don't suppose I helped,' admitted Saxon, 'but I saw him the other day with another girl. He looked happy enough. He'll get over you.'

She looked at him sadly. 'You didn't get over me. Are you suggesting that Giles' love was not as deep as yours?'

'It couldn't be.' His voice was strong and loud, vibrating with confidence. 'Nothing could be. I love you with all the breath in my body, Jancy. If Giles had truly loved you he would never have let you go. He would have fought. He would have staked his claim just as I tried to do. What sickens me is the thought that that man has had your body—and yet I have only myself to blame.'

'No, Saxon.' Jancy smiled serenely. 'Giles never did any more than kiss me. I think he always knew that he did not get my total response. But his love was different. He wanted *me* to be happy, he didn't care about himself. That was why he let me go.'

'He's a fool,' said Saxon softly.

'No, he's a good man. When you cast me out of your life you thought only of yourself. You wouldn't listen to me when I tried to explain about that silly bet, you wouldn't even listen on the *Ocean Queen* when I tried to tell you I loved you. You even took Debra Forrester out. You've no idea how much that hurt.'

He frowned, suddenly puzzled. 'Debra? I don't touch married women.'

'Do you deny that you spent the day with her in Puerto Rico? I was watching for Mrs Fairfax's return and couldn't help seeing you. I wished I hadn't.'

'Heavens,' he laughed. 'I'd have explained if you'd asked me. I'd been for a walk. She saw me heading back and offered me a lift. It's as simple as that.'

'She fancied you,' said Jancy sadly. 'You've no idea how often she sang your praises.'

He grinned. 'It's an occupational hazard having half the women on board fall in love with you. But there was only ever one woman for me, and if that incident on the lifeboat brought you to your senses then it was worth every minute of the agony I suffered.

'And it was agony. No one wanted to let me go on that fishing boat first. I'm no sailor and didn't really know what I was doing, but my job is to save lives and there were men hurt and dying. Every second counted.'

'You could have died yourself,' said Jancy. 'If you had I'd have thrown myself in after you.'

'But it didn't happen,' he said. 'I'm very much alive, and oh, my Jancy, I want to marry you now—today—tomorrow.' He patted his pocket. 'I have a special licence.'

'You were that sure?'

He shook his head wryly. 'I was afraid,

desperately afraid. This was my one last chance. But I knew there was still a way I could make you answer to me. It never fails to work, does it? Right from that first time I kissed you at Phil's engagement party you responded. It's something special we have between us. Something we shall treasure for the rest of our lives.'

Jancy nodded. 'You're a very special man, Saxon. Please hold me tight and never let me go again.'

'There's no fear of that,' he said gravely. 'I'll bind you to me with bands of steel if necessary. You're mine, Jancy. Mine for all time.'

Jancy felt a glow of pride at his words. She was Saxon's woman. Yes, that was what she had wanted from the moment they met. She had never thought it would happen. It was a miracle that it had. But she would make him happy. Oh, yes, she would. There was no doubt about that. Together they would be the happiest couple in the world.

ROMANCE

Next month's romances from Mills & Boon

Each month, you can choose from a world of variety in romance with Mills & Boon. These are the new titles to look out for next month.

LOVE ME NOT Lindsay Armstrong
THE WINTER HEART Lillian Cheatham
DESIRE FOR REVENGE Penny Jordan
AN ALL-CONSUMING PASSION Anne Mather
KNIGHT'S POSSESSION Carole Mortimer
THE COUNTERFEIT SECRETARY Susan Napier
SUNSTROKE Elizabeth Oldfield
BEST LAID PLANS Rosemary Schneider
DANGEROUS MOONLIGHT Kay Thorpe
A MOMENT IN TIME Yvonne Whittal
*__FROM THIS DAY FORWARD__ Sandra Marton
*__THAT MAN FROM TEXAS__ Quinn Wilder

Buy them from your usual paperback stockist, or write to: Mills & Boon Reader Service, P.O. Box 236, Thornton Rd, Croydon, Surrey CR9 3RU, England. Readers in South Africa write to: Mills & Boon Reader Service of Southern Africa, Private Bag X3010, Randburg, 2125.

*These two titles are available *only* from Mills & Boon Reader Service.

Mills & Boon
the rose of romance

ROMANCE

Variety is the spice of romance

Each month, Mills & Boon publish new romances. New stories about people falling in love. A world of variety in romance — from the best writers in the romantic world. Choose from these titles in January.

STRANGER IN TOWN Kerry Allyne
TO FILL A SILENCE Jayne Bauling
SECRET LOVER Kathryn Cranmer
WHAT'S RIGHT Melinda Cross
STORM Vanessa Grant
LOSER TAKE ALL Rosemary Hammond
ONE DREAM ONLY Claudia Jameson
EXPLOSIVE MEETING Charlotte Lamb
SECOND ENCOUNTER Margaret Mayo
ELUSIVE PARADISE Lilian Peake
*****ASK ME NO QUESTIONS** Valerie Parv
*****TO BRING YOU JOY** Essie Summers

On sale where you buy paperbacks. If you require further information or have any difficulty obtaining them, write to: Mills & Boon Reader Service, PO Box 236, Thornton Road, Croydon, Surrey CR9 3RU, England.

*These two titles are available *only* from Mills & Boon Reader Service.

Mills & Boon
the rose of romance